The Sparrow

Under His Wings Trilogy
Book 1

by

Ronna Bacon

The Dedication

To my Mother, Helen Marie Jackson Bacon, who instilled in me a love of reading and challenged me to follow my dream of writing a novel with the words "Why don't you?". Mom, this is for you. Wish you were here today.

Matthew 10:31 "So do not fear; you are more valuable than many sparrows."

Luke 12:6 "Are not five sparrows sold for two cents? Yet not one of them is forgotten before God."

Table of Contents

THE SPARROW

Prologue

A black-clothed form snuck down the hallway of the seniors' home. He peered around a corner, making sure the nurses and other staff were busy. Seeing his way clear, he rounded the corner, making for Room 1121.

He stopped at the door and listened. Silence met his ear. He softly opened the door and slipped through, a dark shadow in the dim light. He stopped and stooped over the form in the bed. Good, she was asleep. Let's just hope she stays that way, he thought, and that the drawers don't creak.

He crept on silent rubber-shod feet to the table in the corner. Carefully opening the drawer, he felt around. Drawing out the papers, he flipped through them. Yes—here was the financial information he needed. Another quick search found a signature. He quickly stuffed the papers in his pocket, stilling at movement from the bed. He slanted his eyes that way. She was still asleep.

Creeping from the room, he managed to make his way back out without being seen. He had the information he needed. Now he could complete his work for the Mastermind.

He slid into his car and started it, creeping away at low speed. He didn't want to get stopped for speeding. He sent a quick text that he had what he needed and sent it the Boss.

Once he was at the bed and breakfast, he pulled out the papers. Something was missing. He frantically searched for the encrypted message. It was not there. His mind raced, trying to figure where he had lost it and couldn't. The Mastermind would not be pleased, but he would make sure the Mastermind never found out.

Now to get to work. He would have to leave for a few days but he would be back. What he needed was at his own place in the nearby city.

Chapter 1

The rain was slanted sideways and cold as it hit her face. She shivered and ducked her head lower but it didn't make any difference. She was soaked. And cold. And was sure she heard footsteps behind her. It would do no good to turn—she couldn't see anything for the rain and the darkness.

She reached for the door and then screamed as a hand came out of the darkness and took hold of the handle. She jumped back and looked up. It was a stranger, but she felt she knew him. She darted through the door and into the dining room and then through to a private dining room. She was scared. Too many things had been happening lately for her not to be.

She kept going through into the kitchen, past the staff busy with the meals for the evening diners and then to the back door. Opening it slowly, she looked around. It seemed clear. So far, so good. Now she just had to make it out of town and she hoped to be safe.

She splashed through the rain and puddles to her truck, hitting the lock just as she reached it. Scrambling inside, her hands shaking so badly she could hardly fit the key into the ignition, she fired up the engine and then put the truck into gear. She drove forward, desperately looking around for anyone who didn't belong.

She screamed and hit the brakes as a figure stepped into her path. She twisted the wheel and then hit the accelerator, the truck fishtailing in the wet. It was not the same man who had been in the restaurant but she was too scared to stop. Panicked, she drove through the barrier and then onto the road. Lights appeared in her rearview mirror.

Swerving on to the road, she sped through town, turning right and left, hoping that whoever was behind her was totally lost. There were no more lights in her mirror. She took the next right and hit the highway out of town. The rain was still coming down in torrents and she could tell the temperature was dropping. Without taking her eyes off the road, she reached over and hit the heater switch, flooding the cab with welcome warmth.

She slowed and then made a left turn. She had to be careful. The road was slick with mud and fallen leaves and it would take just one brief falter in her attention to the it and she would be off into the woods. She crept along as fast as she dared, checking frequently in her mirror for lights.

Then, it happened. She saw a flash of light in front of her and without thinking hit the brakes. The truck fishtailed and then slid off into the deep ditch. She tried frantically to bring the truck under control but it was too late. She felt the crunch of the truck hitting thick trees, the feel of the airbags going off and then nothing.

****

Joshua Logan picked himself up out of the puddles and shook his hands to rid them of the water. He ran for his SUV, digging his keys out and unlocking the vehicle as he slid to a stop. Yanking open the door, he slid in and once the motor was running, spun out of his parking slot and out on the road. He caught a glimpse of red lights and raced towards them. He had to admire Laycee Bradley. She sure seemed to know what she was doing. Wipers working at full speed, he followed her, far enough back that he wouldn't alarm her. He had a pretty good idea where she was headed and though he wouldn't get ahead of her to cut her off, he could follow her. He knew there was a cottage close that the Bradley family used. Not many people knew about it.

He turned on to the same winding narrow track that Laycee had taken. Suddenly he slammed on his brakes. Yes - there were tail lights in the ditch. Defensive driving took over and he was able to stop safely. He leapt from his vehicle and ran to her door. Wrenching it open, he noticed she was not moving. He reached across her and undid her seat belt and then checked her for injuries. Her face had redness and bruising and he knew she had to be in some pain from the seat belt. No bleeding. No broken bones. God looked after her, he thought. He carefully lifted her out and headed to his SUV. By the time they were there, Laycee was soaked. He grabbed a blanket from the back seat and wrapped her snuggly in it, set her on the seat and fastened her in with the seat belt.

Laycee Bradley stirred. Something wasn't right, she thought. She tried to move but couldn't. She could hear a voice beside her. Opening her eyes, she struggled to focus. Joshua's face came into focus.

"Joshua," she whispered. "It's you. I thought it was someone else after me."

"There is," he replied. "We need to get you out of here. Is there anything in your truck you need? Anything hidden anywhere in it? I know how you like to hide things to keep them safe."

She thought and then said, "I have a bag behind the seat. Under my seat, tucked up, there's a brown envelope. Make sure you get that. I can't think..." Her voice faded and her eyes closed.

Joshua took a look at her and then shut the door as softly as he could. He ran back to the truck, fished around under the driver's seat and found the envelope. He pulled out the bag she mentioned, took the keys and made sure nothing else was left. He knew he would have to call his brother, the police chief for the area, but that could wait until they were safe.

He headed his truck away from the site, knowing the rain would wash away any evidence of another vehicle. Laycee was being chased, followed by who knows who, and he didn't want anyone knowing where she was until he could make sure she was safe.

Chapter 2

Joshua reached up into the kitchen cupboard and pulled out his favourite mug, filling it with fresh coffee. After adding cream and sugar to how he liked it, he wrapped his fingers around it, relishing the heat. It may be September on the calendar but it was cold and dreary, with a dampness that went to the bones. He stopped and touched the pictures of his family on the wall in the sunroom — his parents, his brother and his family. How was he ever going to explain what he had gotten himself into when he didn't even know himself?

Leaving the kitchen, he wandered through his home to the living room. The only real light came from the fireplace that was spreading warmth and comfort. He stopped to check the logs; no, he didn't need to add one yet. He straightened the pictures on the mantle. He knew he was just putting in time, time that neither he nor Laycee had, he felt.

He turned and halted beside the couch, looking down at Laycee still sleeping. She had not stirred at all when he laid her there, still bundled up in the blanket from the truck. He nudged the blanket up a bit higher around her neck, brushing the black curls away from her face as he did so. The bruises on her face were more prominent now. What have you gotten into, Laycee? He asked himself. And how can I help? You don't like to have help, but you are so far over your head right now you need it.

—

He continued his path to the large picture window at the front of the house, standing to the side and pulling the drapes back a bit to see out. It was still pitch black and raining. He couldn't tell if anyone was out there, but he still felt uncomfortable, as if someone knew where they were and was just waiting for the right time.

Turning, he returned to the chair he had been sitting in before he went to refill his coffee. Setting the large brown ironstone mug on the table, he settled further back in his favourite chair. It wasn't much to look at but it was old and comfortable. It had been his grandfather's chair and many memories were associated with it. The best memories were the Bible stories and verses his grandfather had shared and the prayers he had put to heaven for his family. Joshua so wished his grandfather was still there to pray for them now. He really needed the prayers of a warrior to get through what he feared was coming.

Picking up his Bible, he spent time in reading and prayer, seeking for wisdom and courage. He needed this time to prepare, but what was he preparing for?

He tugged out a pad of paper and pen from the table drawer and started to list what he knew. He was a carpenter not a detective but knew facts were what mattered. He liked facts. Now to start — where?

****

"I paid you to find her and bring her to me." The voice on the phone was shaking in rage. "What went wrong?"

Tom Brown ran his hand through what hair he had and wished for the hundredth time he had never heard this voice. He had no idea who it was; contact was always by phone and untraceable for him.

"She was spooked. She couldn't have seen us, but she ran. She must have had help, she has totally disappeared. No sign of her or her truck."

"Find her!" Tom shuddered at the venom in the voice. "If you fail, you will be the next statistic and I will find someone else."

The phone clicked off angrily in his ear. Tom blew out a breath and then looked at his brother Andy, who was staring at the floor, watching ants move across the stickiness. They weren't cleaners and really didn't care about the mess and garbage strewn through the house. They weren't home much, any way.

"Any ideas?" Andy asked.

"No!" Tom was short with his brother. He didn't like the situation. They were small time crooks, into break and enters and shop lifting. How had they been found and why had he ever agreed? Money—that had to be it. They needed money to live.

Tom suddenly spun and pointed at Andy. "Who was that guy that followed her? Maybe he has her. Did you get a glimpse of his vehicle?"

Andy shrugged, not really caring about anything at the moment. He had done a lot of drinking when they came back after their failed attempt and his brain just didn't want to work. "No, unless it's someone related to her."

"We need to find out." Tom angrily threw a bottle across the room, watching it shatter on the wall. "We will have to stake out her brothers and see if they lead us anywhere. I'm not ready to die for this yet."

Tom slammed the door on his way to his car. It was an old rusty car and just barely ran but it was all he could afford. Shutting the door took effort as the hinges weren't great. He picked up the papers sitting on the passenger seat and thumbed through them. Yep, he thought, one of the brothers, but which one? He turned the key and the motor reluctantly came to life. He pulled away from the curb, leaving a trail of black smoke and headed for one of the brothers' homes. Now came the part he hated — being patient.

Chapter 3

Joshua tapped the end of the pen on the tablet, then stopped, glancing over at Laycee to make sure the slight noise had not awakened her. It hadn't.

He started his list:

Lacyee is running — why?

Who is after her?

Is it work or personal?

Is it because of someone else?

He flipped the page and started describing the scene from the night before and what all he could remember of the men and the vehicle. It wasn't much. The weather had made it very difficult to see much and he had been more focused on making sure Laycee was fine.

He dropped the tablet to his knee, acknowledging he knew very little. Leaning his head back, he uttered a prayer for wisdom and guidance. Opening his eyes, he glanced over to the couch. Laycee was stirring.

Laycee slowly twisted under the blankets. She was stirring, in that state between sleep and being awake. She was sore all over and when she felt her face, it hurt. Her eyes didn't want to open but she managed to crack them. A fire flickered in her vision. Where was she? She wondered. It was not her home — she didn't have a fireplace.

Movement came into her line of sight and she shoved herself backwards, stopping when she ran out of room. Her eyes flew open. Who was that? Surely not one of the men who had dogged her steps for the last three weeks, showing up wherever she was, following her vehicle. She felt the panic rising within her, and she desperately searched for a way to escape.

Joshua crouched down into her line of sight. He waited for her to speak, but he could see the panic and fear welling up in her.

"It's okay, Laycee." He spoke in a soft voice. "You're safe. I won't let anyone hurt you."

Laycee focused her eyes. "Joshua? It's you?" Her voice was incredulous. "How did I get here? And just where is here?"

"I found you and brought you here. It's my place. Tell you what. Why don't you have a shower and get yourself sorted out? It's late but I can get you something to at least eat and drink if you want."

He reached out a hand to help her up. She hesitated and then took his hand. Gently, he raised her to a sitting position

"Take your time. You'll be dizzy for a bit. There's no rush," he added as she tried to stand.

Dizziness was there and she felt so off balance. She waited for a few minutes and then struggled to her feet. Standing was not a good idea and if it hadn't been for Joshua's strong hands, she would have fallen.

Once she felt steady, he let go of her hands, hovering to make sure she didn't fall.

"The bathroom is just down the hall. There are some samples of shampoo and soap well as a new toothbrush and toothpaste. Towels are on the counter. I also left some clean clothes for you."

She glared at him.

"It's okay. When Caleb and Hannah and the kids come out, sometimes it's really late when they go to leave and the kids are already asleep. Hannah leaves stuff here so they have clean clothes for the next morning. The clothes are hers. She would want you to use them. I think they're about the right size."

Laycee closed her eyes and then apologized. Her mind was not functioning at its usual speed. She knew Hannah from her Bible study group and felt sure Joshua was right. Clothes were clothes and meant to be worn. The whole Logan family were givers, albeit in a quiet, inconspicuous manner.

She untangled her feet from the blanket. Still somewhat unsteady, she managed to make her way to the bathroom. Once inside the room, she was startled when she caught her image in the mirror. Bruises and burns. She could feel the pain from the bruising from the seat belts.

After showering and dressing, she noticed Joshua had left some cream and ibuprofen tablets. Using the cream on her face hurt but then it soothed. She downed a couple of ibuprofen, hoping they would work. She stood for a moment, head down, lost in thought. Why was Joshua helping her? Who was after her? The biggest question was why?

Chapter 4

Joshua heard the click of the bathroom door and turned to face the kitchen doorway. His Golden Retriever, Blues, pushed against him, and he absently rubbed his ears. His mind was racing as to the whys and hows. Somehow, he had to convince Laycee to let him help, keep her brothers updated and out of danger, and find out what was actually going on.

Laycee appeared in the doorway, hesitant about entering. She gave a little half-smile to him. Blues decided it was his turn to take over. He moved over in front of Laycee, sat and then leaned against her. Eyes turned up to her face, a look of absolute adoration planted itself on his face. Laycee laughed and then reached out a hand for Blues to sniff. He licked instead, firmly establishing that Laycee was just all right in his books. She bent and hugged him, so desperate to hug her own dog, a tricoloured Shetland Sheepdog named Defiant. She also so wanted to cuddle with her tuxedo cat, Terror.

"Feeling better?" Joshua asked, as he reached for a mug to pour her a coffee. He handed it to her and indicated where the cream and sugar was.

"I am. Thank you." Laycee pulled out a chair at the round oak table and sat. She played with the edge of the placemat, not sure what to say or if to say anything at all.

"What would you like, Laycee, some toast or something different?" Joshua kept a sideways watch on her, not sure either if he should be saying anything about what happened.

"Toast is fine. Do you have whole wheat or a grain bread?"

"I do. One or two pieces?"

"One I think for now."

After he had the piece of toast on a plate and in front of her, with a selection of butter, jam, cheese spread and peanut butter, he refilled his coffee cup and took a seat at the opposite side of the table from her.

Laycee avoided his eyes, instead glancing around the kitchen. She liked the off white cabinets, the mottled brown and cream countertop. White appliances, she thought—nice. I like that. There was not a lot of clutter on the countertop, but she could tell the kitchen was well used and often. Apparently Joshua liked to cook.

"Laycee," Joshua spoke in a soft voice, "we need to talk about what happened."

Laycee shot a look at him and then turned her attention to her toast. Blues leaned hard against her leg, chin on her thigh. She looked down at him and laughed. He was drooling, wanting some of her toast. She didn't know if he was allowed some, so she ignored him.

"What do we need to talk about?" she asked, delaying the inevitable questions and thoughts she wanted to avoid.

"First, why were you being chased? Who is after you?"

"I don't know," she replied. "I really don't know. I'm a secretary, not working on some big hush-hush project. I'm not in law enforcement so that someone would be after me because of that. I don't know." Her voice rose as she spoke, showing how much it had affected her.

"Okay." Joshua watched her, noting the way she avoided his eyes, the way she ran her fingers through her shoulder-length black curls. He reined in his thought of how he would like to do the same. "So we need to figure this out."

"We?" she cried. "No, I can't let you. I just can't let anyone else get hurt." Her face paled in fright as she imagined what could happen. "I don't know. I am just so afraid. I can't think of who would be after me."

Dropping her piece of toast, she jumped from the table and almost ran into the living room. Joshua dropped his head into his hands and breathed a quick prayer for guidance. God knew what was happening; they had to trust Him at a time when trust seemed to hard.

Following at a slower pace, Joshua entered the room to see Laycee standing staring at the fire. One hand gripped the mantle so tight her knuckles were white. What had scared her so bad? What was it or who was it?

Chapter 5

The sudden, unexpected trilling of music startled both. Laycee jerked, her hand knocking over pictures on the mantle. Joshua reached to steady her, then withdrew his hand.

"That's my phone! That's Liam's ring tone. Where's my phone?" Laycee's eyes searched for her bag, wanting so much to speak with her older brother. He could be a pain at time, too protective, but he was always there when she needed him. And this was one time she really needed him.

"Here's your knapsack." Joshua handed her the bag he had retrieved from her truck.

Her hands shaking, Laycee unzipped the bag and felt for her phone. It had stopped ringing by the time she found it. She saw that a voice mail had come through and dialed her number. It was Liam.

"Where are you, Laycee? Why don't you answer?" She could hear almost panic in her brother's normally calm voice. "You're not home. The police have called. There was a break-in at your house and it has been trashed. Call me. Let me know you're okay."

The phone rang again and she almost dropped it. She answered and breathed a sigh of relief when she heard Liam's voice.

"Laycee - where are you? Are you okay?"

"Liam, I had an accident..."

"An accident? Where are you? Which hospital? I am on my way!" She could hear his keys hitting the door as he headed for his vehicle.

"No, Liam, don't. I'm okay. I'm not in a hospital. A friend found me and is looking after me."

"A friend?" Liam's voice rose to a shout. "Who and where? I'm coming to find you."

"Liam, no. It's not safe. Someone is after me and I don't know who." At this point, her voice was breaking and she could feel tears in the back of her throat. She angrily swiped at her eyes.

Joshua watched, compassion and caring in his gaze. He knew how it would feel if it was his sister.

"Laycee, I don't care. Tell me where you are."

"No, I won't!"

Joshua reached and took her phone, then pushed her gently down into his chair.

"Liam," he spoke into the phone. "It's Joshua Logan. I found Laycee and she's with me. Someone is really after her and she is afraid they may be looking for her through you and Leith."

"Joshua - what, why, how? Okay, let me get this straight. Laycee is running, has an accident, and you just happen to find her? Where is she?"

"She's with me, I said. We need to meet somewhere to talk, but it has to be somewhere safe. I am not sure where, though."

Joshua looked over at Laycee, who was vigorously shaking her head.

"Can I get back to you with a place, Liam? Laycee's safe for now. I think I know of somewhere but I need to check first. You need to be thinking of a place as well. This may come back on you and Leith, so make sure he's in the loop."

There was silence on the phone. Then Liam spoke, his voice more subdued, "It's that bad? I didn't know. I…I…I just want to make sure Laycee's safe. It scared me when the police called and said her place had been trashed and she was nowhere around."

"Give me 30 minutes and I'll call you back."

Joshua clicked off the phone, then stared at it as he turned it over and over in his hand, a thoughtful look on his face. He could feel the palpable fear and anger coming from Laycee. Where to go and who to trust?

Laycee stomped over to the window and cracked open the heavy, floor to window, dark blue drapes. She knew Joshua lived out in the boonies, as she called it, but didn't realize how open around the house it was. Brush was cleared back far from the house, as best she could see in the dark. There were motion sensor lights up and from what he had said in the past, a really good security system. She figured something in his past had dictated this but she didn't know him well enough to ask. Was now the time to do so?

Joshua looked up from his phone and watched Laycee. There was so much he wanted to say. He had been a silent observer for years, wanting to get to know her better, but not sure how to. He felt he knew so little about her other than she had a strong faith in God. Would that faith hold? He knew his would be tested over and over during the next few days, at least, he hoped it would be days, not weeks. Hours would be even better.

"Laycee. We need to come up with a plan. We can't wing it any more. Whoever is after you will be following Liam and Leith. They may even be outside if they happened to see my SUV."

Laycee shook her head. "No, I can't meet them. I can't bring danger to them."

"Laycee, it's already there. They were probably watching your place and saw Liam there. They probably already know you have two brothers and know their activities and schedules. What we need to do is try and figure out who and why."

Laycee turned to face him, letting the drapes fall back in to place. Her eyes were shining with tears and traces of tears tracked across her cheeks. She drew in a shaky breath.

"All right, then, what do you suggest? And just because you suggest it, doesn't mean it happens." Joshua grinned at her feistiness. "And wipe that grin off your face, buster."

Now that was the Laycee he knew— ready to face the world and conquer it.

"First, we pray." He reached out a hand and she hesitantly took it. His warm firm grasp helped to steady her.

"Father, You know what's going on. You know the fear Laycee is facing. You are in control. Lead us with Your wisdom. Help us to plan and follow You. Remind us that we are more important to You than a sparrow. Give us the strength we need.

Provide protection for those we love and for ourselves. Amen."

Chapter 6

Laycee stood for a minute, wrapped in the knowledge that God was in control and that He really did care what happened. She raised her eyes, meeting Joshua's. She hesitated, trying to figure out the look in his eyes.

"Where do we go from here?" She asked.

"First, we have to have something more to eat. Who knows when we well next eat. I also want to pack up some food and drinks to take with us. Then I need to get Blues ready to go. We may need him."

"I can look after the food. Do what you need to do." Laycee turned and headed for the kitchen.

Joshua looked after her for a minute, shook his head and headed for his bedroom. A quick shower, change of clothes, a packsack stuffed with what he needed from there, and he was ready to go. He stopped in the hallway, dropped his pack, and pulled out the saddlebags he used for Blues. He made sure the supplies were still there: maps, flashlight, batteries, first aid kit, whatever he needed on his search and rescue treks.

He stopped at the pantry and filled another pack with food and water bottles as well as the collapsible dishes for Blues. When he turned to the kitchen, he saw that Laycee had made sandwiches, pulled out apples and oranges, and water and juice, and was stuffing another pack with them. She was also pulling out spare clear bags and markers and stuffing them in too.

"Why the bags and markers?" he asked.

"Evidence. If we find anything, we need to put it in something," she replied, not looking up from her task.

"But we're not the police. It won't be accepted as evidence."

"I don't care. I need to do this. If we find something, we'll call in the police, but I am not sure who I can trust."

"We can call Caleb. He's the law, he can help."

"Sure, but if we can't reach him, then what?" Laycee argued back.

"We'll keep trying. We'll figure it out." Joshua cocked his head to the right and studied her. She was too calm, taking it too silently. She was ready to break and he knew it was coming. What would be the tipoff?

Laycee's hands stilled. She dropped the snacks she was holding and her hands flew to her mouth. Tears welled in her eyes.

"Defiant. Terror. Where are they? Are they all right? I have to get home. I have to find them. I need them. They need me!" Her voice rose with each word, fear evident in her voice. She turned for the door, then stopped. She ran at Joshua, pounding at him. "You need to take me home. I need to go home. I need to find them!"

Joshua gripped her upper arms, trying to stop her fists. When that didn't work, he simply wrapped his arms around her and held her. Her fists stopped and her fingers clutched into his plaid work shirt, tightening until the knuckles were white. He could feel the dampness on his shirt. He didn't care. She needed the tears, she needed the hug.

When her shaking had stopped and he could hear just broken breaths, he set her back from him and dipping his head, looked into her eyes.

"We'll find them. Let me call Liam and see where they are. He'll know. He was at your home with the police." He waited until she finally gave a small nod, then reached for his phone.

Dialing Liam's number, he asked as soon as Liam answered, "Laycee needs to know where her pets are. She's starting to panic."

"Leith has them. He's taking them to Doc Victor. Doc was willing to open up his office to check them out, then Leith was going to take them with him. They seem fine, just real clingy, more than usual." Joshua could hear the eye roll in that sentence. He knew from Liam that Laycee and her animals were inseparable, that where one was in the house, they all were. It would have been devastating to Laycee if something happened to either one. "I found Terror tucked away in a corner of the closet. She wasn't too happy about me digging her out. Defiant was still in his crate. Laycee always covers it part way, so the vandals may not have seen him, or else decided he didn't matter."

Joshua tilted the phone away from his mouth and reassured Laycee that the pets were fine, that her brother had them and was taking care of them.

Putting the phone back to his mouth, he asked, "Have you come up with a spot to meet yet? We're getting ready to leave and need to know where to find you."

"There's an old hunt camp back a ways from your place. Here are the directions. Laycee knows where it is, if she can keep her head straight." Joshua snickered, knowing that Liam was being sarcastic. Of all of them, Laycee was the one with the best memory, who could always be depended on to keep everyone and everything straight and in line. "Make sure you're not followed. Turn off your location on both your phones before you leave. I'm doing the same. Not sure if the goons after Laycee have our numbers but chances are they do, having tossed her place."

"We'll do that. Leaving soon. If something happens, I'll send a text."

Joshua touched his phone and turned off the location application. He then reached for Laycee's and did the same. She watched in silence, emotions spent.

"All right, let's hit the road," Joshua scooped up backpacks and Blues' leash. Blues headed for the door. Turning off lights on the way to the door, he stopped and keyed in his password for the security system. He put a hand out to Laycee to keep her inside.

"Wait. I'll put the stuff and Blues in first and then come back." Quickly following through on his word, he came back, took Laycee's hand, rekeyed in his password and locked the door. He helped Laycee in the SUV and then keyed the motor to life. He took a look around in the dark, wondering if they were being watched, and also wondering when he would

---

31

see his place again. Work could wait. He was held up anyway on his renovation job right now waiting for material and trim.   The customer was understanding, and Joshua had looked at this time as a short vacation. Vacation it was not, but friends were more important.

Liam tapped his fingers on the steering wheel, deep in thought. Who was after his sister? She was a secretary, did volunteer work in a senior's home, and didn't have any enemies, at least none that he knew of. It was just too bizarre. He knew her employer, a physician, who was an upstanding member of the community and of their church. Nothing about him screamed problem or danger. His own work as a landscaper certainly didn't bring danger to either Laycee or Leith and Leith was a tile setter; nothing there seemed out of place. Joshua—he knew him, not well, but enough to know that he was a compassionate, caring person. Leith likely knew him better, having worked on Joshua's renovation projects.

He picked up his phone and dialed Leith's number.

When Leith answered, his first question was about Laycee's animals.

"Doc Victor says they're okay. Shaken, scared, but not hurt in any way. Defiant will be sticking a lot closer to Laycee now though, given the separation anxiety Shelties are known for. Terror is Terror— she'll be okay as well."

"That's a relief. Laycee just about lost it, Joshua said, when she remembered they were home when the break-in happened."

"Did Caleb say if anything was missing that he could see?"

"Not that he knew of, but then, it would take Laycee to know. She knows exactly where everything in and if someone has touched something of hers."

"That she does. Remember all those times we messed with her, moving or just touching something?"

"Yeah. I can remember Mom lighting into us for that. It was fun, though, at the time." Liam sighed. "I just wish I knew what was going on right now, what Laycee had gotten mixed up in."

"Me, too. That's our sister that they're after. I want a piece of them. I can't think of anything that she's mentioned lately that might be a clue."

"Nor me. I.." Liam's voice trailed away.

"What? Did you think of something?"

"Yeah. She mentioned about six weeks ago that something seemed wrong with the lady she was visiting with. Defiant wanted to really snuggle up and cling to her, almost as if he sensed something. Laycee just shrugged it off. Apparently, the lady died a week or so later, and Laycee though Defiant had picked up on that."

"That's worth mentioning to Caleb. Do you know the name?"

"No, but I'm to meet Laycee and Joshua in a bit. I won't tell you where, but I will call once we're together and we can think it through, all four of us.

Let Caleb know that Laycee is safe, but not where she is."

"Will do. Be careful, brother. In my prayers. This is when I wish Mom and Dad were still here, our prayer warriors."

"I know. I miss that. Sometimes, I really need their prayers."

Liam clicked off his phone, and then turned off the location app. He didn't think he was being followed but took a circuitous route to the hunt camp.

Dawn was breaking as he turned into the narrow, tree-canopied lane. Undergrowth brushed against his truck as he crept down towards the camp. He peered through the windshield. No tracks. Good. That must mean that he was first or that no one knew where they were.

He parked before he reached the camp and turning off the vehicle, he stepped out and closed the door, locking it before he did so. He didn't want the sound of the key fob beep to alert anyone around.

He stepped carefully forward, making sure of what was under each foot before he set his weight on it. When he spied the camp, he stopped at the edge of the woods and looked around. It seemed okay, but he waited. No movement at all.

He then proceeded across the short distance to the back door. Unlocking it, he swung the door open and stepped to one side. Nothing. He stepped inside. It was the same as when he was last there about six weeks ago. Good. Now to wait for Laycee and Joshua. He refused to light a fire—it would be a dead giveaway that someone was there.

—

A slight noise sent him to the side of the door. He waited. Hushed footsteps approached, two people by the sound of it. The footsteps stopped. He waited. Then a form entered the room. He waited. When the light hit, he breathed easier and spoke.

"Joshua."

Joshua spun around in surprise.

"Liam. You're here."

"Where's Laycee?"

Laycee stepped through the door and into her big brother's embrace. His bear hug was tight and her arms clasped him just as tight. Moments passed before they moved back and looked into each other's faces.

"Ouch." Liam's fingers traced the bruises and redness on her face.

Laycee smacked his arm. "Is that all you can say, ouch?"

Liam smirked. "Well, yeah! What else do you want me to say?"

Laycee huffed and turned her back on him. Joshua caught the look on her face and the tears in her eyes and exchanged a look with Liam.

Liam placed his hands on her shoulders. "I'm glad you're okay. You had me worried."

Laycee stood still for a moment and then moved away to stand at the desk in the corner of the room.

"Do you remember Grand-dad working here? He always would stop and spend time with us, no matter how busy he was with the books and records."

Liam knew she was avoiding the questions he wanted to ask, buying time to get her emotions back in control.

"I do. Both sets of grandparents always had time for us. They helped mold us to who we are today."

"That they did."

Laycee turned, eyes flying around the room, taking in everything. Everything looked the same, but she wasn't. The night had changed her and not for the good, she thought. She moved from desk to table to kitchen to fireplace to bookshelf.

At the bookshelf, she stopped. Something was different. Someone had been here and moved books around. Who would have been here?

"Liam, did you move the books around when you were here last?" she asked.

Liam's look changed and he strode across the room to stand beside her. Laycee was tall for a woman, 5'8" but Liam seemed to tower over her tonight, his 6'2" frame lean and strong.

"No, I didn't. What's different about the shelf?"

Joshua was beside the siblings, taking in their looks. Both were tall and lithe. Black hair was curly and he knew both had brown eyes. Their facial features were so similar, anyone would know they were brother and sister, and he knew Leith looked like them, except for having hazel eyes. This could be a problem. They were a close knit family and if you hurt one, you hurt all three.

"The books have been moved. I thought we were the only ones who had keys to the place now."

"We are."

Liam strode to the doors and took a look at the locks. Nothing seemed odd about them, no scratches or signs that they had been broken into. Windows were the same. Strange.

Lacyee moved the books back to where they should be. She stopped with the last book in her hand. Something made her open it. Inside was an envelope that had not been there the last time she read it.

Her eyes flew up, meeting Joshua's and then moving to Liam. She tilted the book and showed them. Both men moved towards her and Liam reached for the book.

The long white envelope was not marked in any way. From the medicine cabinet in the bathroom, Joshua dug out some tweezers, then used them to pick up the envelope. Placing it on the table, he checked out the front and then flipped it over. It wasn't sealed. He pulled back the flap and then pulled out the folded sheet of paper inside. Just an ordinary sheet of copy paper, it seemed.

He unfolded it and then stopped. Laycee and Liam crowded around him, reading the numbers. Eyes flew to each other's. What had they stepped into?

Joshua pulled out his phone and took a picture of the letter. He then sent an email to his brother, Caleb, with the photo attached. Caleb needed to know. No matter what Laycee said, law enforcement had to now get involved.

Chapter 8

Caleb Logan closed his Bible and rubbed his hand across the worn leather cover, deep in thought. His mind sometimes had trouble grasping the concept that God cared so much, when he saw so much destruction in his career. Being a police officer had gotten more and more difficult and dangerous. He picked up his mug of tea and wandered over to the French door overlooking the backyard. Liam had done a wonderful job on it; the mixtures of flowers and hard surfaces were amazing. He could faintly hear the tinkle of the waterfall through the glass.

He felt a hand on his side and reached around to hug his wife, Hannah, to him. He was blessed. He was blessed with such a sweet wife who understood how important he felt his work was and with two sons who loved him and couldn't wait to share their adventures with him. Steam rising from her flavoured coffee mixed with the scent of his herbal tea. They stood for a while, just enjoying the early morning and being together. All too soon, he would be off and she would be busy with the rambunctious preschoolers they called their sons.

Caleb's phone vibrated and he sighed. All too early, someone was looking for him. Hannah took his mug as he reached for his phone.

"It's from Joshua," he stated. "Now I wonder what's up. Liam seemed to think he and Laycee were in some sort of trouble last night."

"I hope he's okay," Hannah responded, a worried look creeping into her eyes.

Caleb brought up the text Joshua and sent and read it. He tensed and then read through the text again. Just what have you gotten into, Joshua, he wondered. How deep in this going to get?

"Is everything okay?" He faintly heard Hannah's voice.

Dragging his thoughts back from the text, he nodded. "I think so. Just keep us in prayer. I don't know where Joshua is right now, but he certainly need protection. He seems to have gotten into something that I don't like and I don't know where he is right now."

Giving Hannah a quick kiss goodbye, Caleb strode for the door and to his unmarked SUV. His mind kept replying the text message.

Once at his office, he greeted those officers already there on his way to his office. He searched the room and then beckoned at Ben Johnson who was the head of the detective branch of the department. The gray-haired Ben made his way over and joined Caleb.

"Close the door, Ben." Once the door was closed and they were seated, Caleb pulled out his phone. He read the text again and then passed his phone to Ben.

Ben read over and over. His gray eyes was puzzled when he looked up.

"What is this? And why has Joshua sent it to you?"

Caleb ran his fingers through his blond hair and sighed. "Laycee Bradley was targeted by someone last night and Joshua was there. She was in an accident and he has taken her to a safe place until we can figure out who and why."

"That's why she wasn't in her truck when the patrol found it. They have been searching the woods but haven't had any luck."

"Yeah. We need to call them in." He picked up his phone and let the dispatcher know to do just that.

"So now we need to figure out what this is and what it means."

Using his Bluetooth connection, Caleb sent the text to his computer. Ben rose and watched over his shoulder as he brought it up. It seemed even more chilling in larger print:

26 12 12 15

19 15

19 7 7 23 12 25 1 1 22

4 19 16 26

1 10 12

26 1 10 15 24

15 11 12 8 22 19 14

10 1 1 10

Caleb read the figures again, trying to make sense of them. They didn't.

"What on earth?" Ben asked. "What is this all about?"

"I don't know. Unless……". He grabbed his phone and sent a quick text, fingers tapping on the desk.

The phone jingled with the Incoming text.

He looked at it and sighed. Things had gotten only muddier.

"They don't have any idea what this is, either. Some kind of code but what's the key?"

Ben threw a glance at Caleb, back to the phone, and then leaned back against the wall, letting his weight rest on it. "Well, that does it."

Caleb snorted, but he agreed with sentiment. This just got a whole lot bigger than someone after Laycee. What had she stumbled upon?

"So, Caleb, how did that note get into that book in the first place?"

Caleb stilled. A horrifying thought crossed his mind. It had to be someone who knew Laycee, someone who had been at the cabin. He closed his eyes in a silent prayer of protection for the ones there and then picked up his pen, beginning to devise a plan on how to proceed. For once he agreed with Ben— lists were good.

Chapter 9

Liam brought over a fresh cup of coffee and sat at the table across from Joshua. He looked worn. He picked up the plastic bag with the note in and read it once again. It didn't make sense. Just a bunch of numbers.

Joshua looked up from his note pad and then shoved it across the table to Liam, nodding for him to look. He had been listing ideas and people he suspected.

Liam turned it so he could read it. Maybe Joshua had an idea. He was lost. He wanted to protect his sister but against an unknown enemy, how could he?

"I like some of these ideas," he said, "but how do we prove any of them? Laycee hasn't said she has noticed anything out of the ordinary."

"No. I think she has. She just doesn't know it. Something is off, someone is off, and we'll figure it out."

"It had better be before anyone gets hurt." Liam felt himself get more and more angrier. His stomach burned at the thought of his sister being in someone's crosshairs.

The page of numbers sat between the two men, taunting them.

Liam sighed. "It's 6. I need to get going. I have to be on the job today; I can't leave it to my foreman. This client is way too big a deal." He was torn—needing to get to work and needing to stay.

Joshua looked with compassion at his friend. They had known each other pretty well before but this had just added a new dimension to their friendship. He knew Leith was champing at the bit to be with them, but he was out of town today, sourcing material for a renovation he was working on. He wouldn't be back until tomorrow. That meant Joshua would be the one Laycee would have to depend upon, and at the moment, he just wasn't confident that he could protect her against the unknown.

Liam rose and put his mug in the sink. He stepped over the couch where Laycee had stretched out and was asleep. He stood for a few minutes, staring down at her, then reached and tugged the blanket up around her neck. She didn't stir, one hand tucked under the pillow and the other hand curled up under her chin. The bruises were darker, dark in comparison to her ivory skin. He leant over and dropped a quick kiss on her hair and then turned. Lifting a hand to Joshua, he walked out the door and to his vehicle, not knowing what would be coming and not knowing if he would see Laycee that night. He could only leave her with the Lord.

Joshua lifted the paper with the numbers on it again. He knew there was a code but he was too tired to figure it out. His eyes drooped closed and he laid his head on his outstretched arms. Soon the cabin was quiet, except for the click of Blues' nails as he patrolled.

A couple of hours later, Laycee stirred, grimacing at the pain she felt. Her eyelids fluttered as

—

she roused. A rough tongue swiped across her hand and she jumped. Eyes open, she found herself eye to eye with Blues.

He sat, then laid his chin on the couch, almost nose to nose with her. A tongue came out and swiped across her face, catching her mouth. Then he grinned, tongue lolling off to one side, and brown eyes fixed on her.

"Yuck! You just had to do that, didn't you, big boy?" Laycee wiped off her mouth. Blues' head tilted to the side as he listened to her.

Laycee's eyes searched the room, taking in the wide logs of the wall, the worn wide plank flooring, the worn but comfortable furnishings. Many a vacation had been spent here. She remembered her parents and the way they had raised them, the way they made sure there was fun to their lives.

Her eyes continued to move and stopped on Joshua. His head was still on his arms and she could tell he was sound asleep. Moving quietly, she threw back the blanket and sat up.

"That wasn't such a good idea," she said to Blues, as her head spun. Waiting until the world stopped spinning, she stood and made her way to the bathroom. Splashing water on her face, she studied herself in the mirror. She sure wouldn't win any beauty contests, she thought, but then life was more important than that. She looked down, darks thoughts crossing her mind. She just couldn't understand what was happening. Why her?

She stepped quietly back into the kitchen area and moved to make a new pot of coffee. Perhaps that

---

would help to clear her mind, it felt so foggy. She grabbed an apple out of the pack they had brought and turned to the table.

Joshua had awakened and was watching her.

"Feel any better?"

"Some. I think the nap helped." She poured them both fresh mugs of coffee and then sat at the table. She pulled over the note she had found and studied it once again. "Did you and Liam make any headway on this?"

Joshua shook his head. "No. Liam had to leave anyway. He said he would call or text." He looked at Blues who was snuggled in tight to Laycee, head on her knees, eyes closed in sheer delight as she rubbed his ears. "I think I've lost a dog."

Laycee looked down and then grinned. "I always seem to attract dogs. They follow me all over."

Joshua laughed and then looked at the clock.

"Were you to be at the seniors' home today?"

She shook her head. "Not today. I have had to take a break after Mrs. Lang passed away. She was just so special. Do you know if Leith is bringing me my pets?"

It was Joshua's turn to shake his head. "He's out of town today. Liam said they were at his place, but he didn't think we should go there. He figures both their places are being watched."

Laycee closed her eyes in pain. She missed her pets. Defiant was just so much a part of her, she swore he could read her mind. Even with the

———

mischief he got into, the pens and paper he chewed up and spit out, the toys strewn all over the house, he was just too lovable. She needed to hug him and bury her face in his fur. She needed to laugh at Terror, at the way she threw herself around, at her musical trill of a meow/purr combination, her deer-in-the-headlight stare. Soon, she promised, very soon she would be back with them.

Chapter 10

Caleb stared once again at the note. His mind spinning at the possibilities, he was suddenly afraid.

Ben moved to take a seat in one of the arm chairs at the front of his desk, picking up a pad of paper and pen.

"Time to brainstorm. What do we know and what do we suspect?"

Caleb stared across the room at the framed diplomas, commendations and awards. He didn't see them. Hannah had had them framed and hung on the pale cream walls. The dark wood frames matched the trim and wainscoting of his office, which set off the mixed brown carpeting. There was no window, but she had made sure he had good lighting, knowing how many hours he spent there.

Caleb drew his gaze back to Ben His mind was starting to process what was happening, and he didn't like it one bit. That was his brother who was involved in who knew what.

"There are just too many things it can be," he replied. "Laycee seems to be the one everything hinges on, or is that the way we are meant to think?" He spoke slowly as new ideas raised their heads.

Ben started to make a list. He loved lists. He loved to plot scenarios and cross off the ones that didn't work. Caleb had always told him he would have made a good screenwriter but Ben just laughed.

He was where he wanted to be and doing what he loved.

"Okay - so here goes: grandparent scam, drug theft, drug dealing, elder abuse, mediation mixups, employee problems…I guess you're right on this one. We don't have enough information to made a clear decision as to what it is. We need to talk to Laycee."

"I agree but I don't think we'll get her anywhere near us right now. She's running scared, and I can't say I blame her."

"Has Joshua ever said anything in the past about Laycee? I know he volunteers with the search and rescue but does she? Or one of her brothers?"

"That's a good thought. Maybe it has nothing to do with the seniors' home."

Caleb threw his pen down in frustration and leaned back in chair, the black leather creaking. He ran his hands through his hair, his gaze once again going across the room. There had to be something. What were they missing?

Ben took another look at the message. Then he straightened. "You know what this is, don't you?"

Caleb shook his head.

"It's a cryptogram. Letter substitution, I bet. Each number would be a letter." Ben's mind was racing faster than he could speak. "If we can figure out the code, then we might be able to figure out what it is." He jumped to his feet and headed for the door. "I'll let you old folks sit around while us young folks work on it."

—

Caleb laughed and tossed a balled up piece of paper after him, bouncing it off the closing door. Ben might just be right. He picked up his phone and sent a text to Joshua, asking him if they had thought of that.

Then, looking at his desk, he sighed. There was other investigations he needed to work on. He would let the "young folks" struggle with the numbers, he would be busy elsewhere. He shook his head at Ben's joking. Ben was an old-timer on the force and knew when a bit of levity helped. He had a lot to learn and he hoped Ben stayed around while he did.

Bending his head over his paperwork, he become engrossed in it. Time passed. He looked up, startled at the passing of time, when he heard a tap at his door. He stood, opened the door, and faced Liam Bradley. Moving aside, he motioned Liam in and shut the door.

Liam stood and stared at him, sitting when Caleb asked him to have a seat.

"What's going on, Caleb? What do you know?"

Caleb was silent for a moment, then knowing he could be honest with his friend, stated, "I wish I knew, Liam. I really wish I knew. Ben is working on the text; he has an idea it's a cryptogram, but other than that, I really don't know. There are so many possibilities, and I have a couple of detectives tracing Laycee's last few weeks to see if something stands out."

Liam's gaze never left his face. "So we really are at a loss, is that what you're saying?"

"Right now, I would. But I am confident we'll find something soon and be able to unravel the puzzle."

"I hope so." Both men became silent, lost in their thoughts.

****

"What do you mean, you can't find the paper?" The voice hissed through the phone, its very tone sending shivers of fear down the listener's spine.

"I can't. I have no idea where it is. I don't have it. I never had it," he protested.

"Find it. If you don't….." The voice died away with the threat.

Tom shuddered, not wanting to think about what the threat implied. He knew he had to find that paper. If not, he knew he would pay the price.

Andy looked at him and shrugged as if it were not a big deal. Andy had no idea of that was going down. As long as he had a bottle or a fix, he was fine.

The phone clicked angrily in Tom's ear. He threw his at the couch. Now what? He had to find Laycee, but she seemed to have disappeared off the face of the earth.

He grabbed his phone and his keys and jerked his brother to his feet, pushing him out the door ahead of him and to his car. Shoving Andy into the passenger seat, he climbed into the driver's side and started the car.

"Where're we going, Tom?" Andy's words were slurred. Tom knew that he was a liability but he was still his brother. He would need his help at some point, just needed to get him sober.

Tom's car peeled away from the curb and shot out of the subdivision. He drove around aimlessly for a while then decided to park down the street from Laycee's house. Maybe someone would come and he could follow them. At this point, that was all he had, the possibility someone would lead him to her.

****

Ben shoved the door open in excitement, stopping when he saw Liam.

Caleb waved him in. "At this point, Ben, we might as well let Liam know what we know. He's not going anywhere until he does know."

Ben nodded. "I think I've got it figured out. It's a straight substitution, letter for number. Very elementary, in fact. I would think that whoever made it knew it had to be simple."

Caleb's eyes never left Ben's face. "So, what did you come up with?"

Ben sat down in the chair beside Liam. "I am not sure how much you know about cryptogram puzzles, but there is a simple substitution of letter for letter. Say, you want an "A" so you put in "X" as the letter "A". In this case, they have put in numbers for the letters. Once I figured out the vowels, it was easy. Usually once you solve the vowels or common letters, you can figure out what the rest is."

"Okay," Liam said. "That's easy to understand. Now, what does the note say?"

Both men leaned closer to Ben as he pulled out the sheet he had been working on.

"It took me a while to figure out the vowels. I finally got that 19 is A, which meant it had to be a short word, to make any sense; 15 became T. I substituted the 19s and 15s. Then I worked on the numbers that were the same and side by side.

"This is what I got: Meet at Applewood Farm, one month Tuesday, noon."

Caleb sat back. Applewood Farm was just outside town. Contrary to its name, there were no apple trees on it. The name was just something a long-ago owner made up, to spite the fact that apple trees couldn't grow on the land for some reason. Today it was a thriving bed and breakfast inn, which catered to a very select clientele, and offered special deals for events.

"But what Tuesday?" Liam felt like he was asking an overly obvious question.

Ben looked grim. "That's what we need to figure out. And I don't think the owners of the Farm are involved. They've been part of the community and church for years."

Chapter 11

Laycee was tired. She was tired of hurting. She was tired of not being at home. She was tired of hiding. She was just plain tired. She shoved back her chair and stood. Her hand on the door, she stopped. "I'm going outside. I need air. And I don't care if anyone is out there who wants to hurt me. They can't make it any worse." The door slammed behind her.

Joshua jumped at the loud bang. He rose, opened the door, and sent Blues out with her. Blues would alert if anyone was around. He considered Laycee part of his family now and his drive was to protect his own.

Joshua headed back into the kitchen. They needed to eat and soup and sandwiches would be an easy fix. The soup would stay hot until Laycee came back in.

The trilling of his phone caught his attention. Tilting it to look at it, he answered, "Caleb. What have you got?"

"Ben solved the puzzle. What do you know about Applewood Farm? And what does Laycee know?"

Joshua's body stilled. Now it was beginning to make some sense. He had to find Laycee. But where outside was she?

"I'll call you back." Hanging up on Caleb's protest, Joshua headed for the door.

Blues was barking, his angry bark that denoted strangers. Joshua hit the outside in a full run, looking for Laycee and Blues. Around the corner of the cabin, he found Laycee on the ground, not moving. Blues was huddled beside her, not barking now and chin on her back. Joshua hit the ground as a bullet hit the log of the cabin near his head. Somehow, someone had found them. He quickly dialed Caleb's number.

"Caleb, Laycee's down and someone is shooting at us. We're pinned outside the cabin."

Joshua raised his head and looked around. He couldn't see or hear anything. He dragged himself over to Laycee and reached for her. She was breathing. He couldn't see if she was hurt and Blues wouldn't move. Joshua shoved his dog away and then hugged Laycee under one of his arms. If they could make it back into the cabin, they could hide. There was an underground cellar not many people knew. He began to crawl towards the back of the cabin, moving cautiously and stopping every few feet, listening for approaching footsteps or more bullets. Blues crept on his belly beside him and helped to pull Laycee with them. Once they made the back of the cabin, Joshua moved faster. The door was just ahead.

They had made it back inside. He couldn't stop to check on Laycee yet, they had to get to the secret room. He grabbed their backpacks and the letter, snagging their phones too. Everything got stuffed in one of the packs. He reached for the wall, hitting the spot Laycee had told him about. The section of wall moved.

"In you go, Blues." Blues looked at him as if he was nuts and then entered the dark dusty space. Joshua threw in the packs and then turned. He locked the doors and then stooped, gathering Laycee in his arms. He tilted his head. Yes, there were footsteps outside, making their way around the cabin. He stepped into the room after Blues and shoved the wall section back in place. He prayed fervently that whoever was out there either couldn't make it into the cabin or had no idea of a secret room.

****

Caleb sprang to his feet and raced for the door, Ben and Liam on his heels. Barking orders, he ran for the door and his car. He could hear footsteps behind him—Ben and Liam headed for his car, patrol officers headed for their cruisers.

"Give me the address for the cabin," he barked at Liam.

Liam stared at him.

"The address. What is it?"

Liam stuttered as he gave it, his mind going to his sister. He vaguely heard Caleb on his radio giving the address and directing the patrols.

Lights and sirens on, Caleb sped through town, leading a convoy of cruisers. Both Ben and Liam grabbed for support as the car rocketed down the road and around corners.

Caleb sent up prayers, hoping that they would be in time, that both Joshua and Laycee would be safe. He didn't want to face Hannah if something

—

happened to Joshua; Joshua was the brother Hannah had never had and had always wanted. His widow could accept the dangers of his job, but Joshua shouldn't be facing those dangers.

Liam closed his eyes. He couldn't bear to think of what they might face.

Caleb's phone rang. He dug it out and tossed it to Ben, so that he could keep his attention on the road.

"It's Joshua," Ben stated. "A text - they're in a hidden room?" He turned and shot a look at Liam, nodding when Liam's eyes found his and then slid shut. "So far, he says they're safe but Laycee is hurt. He can't see how bad. He doesn't want to put on any light in case someone is in the cabin."

"Get paramedics on the way. When we get there, Liam, you stay back. I don't need you getting the way until we have the situation locked down and safe." Caleb barely spared a glance at his friend as Liam acknowledged this.

Caleb slowed as he neared the turn to the cabin and silenced the siren and turned off the lights. He parked and got out, as did Ben. Liam stood near the cruiser, face drawn and hands clasped.

Caleb drew his men around him and sent them, some to watch the road, others to circle around the cabin. He turned to Ben and motioned him to follow. They disappeared from Liam's sight.

Liam's phone chimed, and he looked down. Leith.

"Hi, Leith."

—

58

"Liam, what's up? Something is, I can tell from your voice."

"There is. Ben solved the cryptogram Laycee found. But there's been a shooting at the cabin and we don't know what all is going on. Joshua got them into the room and now Caleb and his men are on their way in. Joshua said something about Laycee being hurt but I don't know what he means." Liam's voice was breaking and tears gathered in his eyes.

Leith was silent, then "I'm on my way. I'm in town and will be there in 10 minutes."

"Be careful, Leith. We don't know yet who is involved. I feel like I can't trust anyone."

"I hear you." The phone clicked off.

Liam turned his phone over and over in his hands, ready to pitch it at the nearest tree. He wanted, no needed, to be there at the cabin, but knew he had to wait. It wasn't fair. First, their parents were taken far too soon and now Laycee.

Chapter 12

Liam heard a vehicle behind him and a door slam. He turned. Leith had been stopped by a young officer. He jogged over.

"He's my brother. Let him through."

"I'm sorry, sir. I can't do that."

"I'll take the responsibility. That's his sister in that cabin." Liam reached over and pulled Leith to his side. The patrol officer made a move to stop them, then halted at the look on Liam's face. As they walked back to Caleb's car, the officer was on their heels.

"Any word yet?" Leith's face reflected his own, showing the fear, worry and anxiety they both felt.

Liam shook his head and then brought Leith up to date on what they had discovered so far.

Leith looked thoughtful as he stared at Liam, then looked down the lane towards the cabin.

Liam cocked his head and raised an eyebrow. Leith looked at him and then shook his head.

"I'm thinking."

"I know. I can smell the smoke." This was a longstanding joke between the brothers.

"Yeah, right. That's not my brain cells burning, that's yours." He started to say something, then stopped as Liam took a look at the officer standing

———

near them, intently listening to their conversation. "Later."

The brothers stood shoulder to shoulder, side by side, watching for word, almost identical in looks and colouring. The Irish in their ancestry showed through in their colouring. Liam's eyes were brown, Leith's hazel. Both stood over 6', with just a mere fraction of an inch between their heights. Concern was etched on their faces. Their phones both vibrated in their pockets, and after a quick peek, they returned them. Right now, what was important was down that little, narrow, tree-shaded lane that had undergrowth into the track in spaces. Texts and voice mail could wait.

Ben appeared from the trees and beckoned them forward. The young officer jogged ahead and spoke with him, gesturing towards Leith. Ben shot a look at the brothers, then said something to the officer, who in turn jogged back to his car.

Ben waited for the brothers and then spoke.

"It was kids. They thought Blues was a wild dog and they were shooting at him, just for fun." Ben's face showed his anger and frustration. "Caleb needs you to show him the panel to get in. Joshua isn't answering his phone."

The brothers broke into a run and headed for the family cabin. Caleb stood in the doorway, watching as his officers dealt with the youths and searched for evidence. He looked up as the two approached.

"I need to know where the door is. We need to make sure they're okay."

****

Laycee stirred in Joshua's arm. Her eyes opened. She felt safe. But it was so dark. Had she been unconscious for that long? Was she blind? Panic started to rise and she fought to get loose.

Joshua let her go and heard her stumble to her feet, Blues tight to her.

"Laycee, it's okay. We're safe."

"Where are we?"

"Do you remember telling Liam telling me about that secret panel one day we were talking about renegades and the underground railway?" At her nod, he continued, "We're in there. You had gone outside and I heard shooting. I found you and now we're in here until Caleb comes."

"But Caleb won't know where the panel is. How will we know when it's safe?

"Caleb might not know but your brothers do. He'll find out from them."

Laycee moved back toward the sound of his voice and touched his arm. He snugged her up against him under his left arm, leaving the knotted fist of his right hand free. He would do his best to protect her, someone who was becoming very dear to him. He didn't know how she felt, but he wanted to pursue this once events had finished and she was once again safe from the unknown.

"Do you know how long we've been in here?" Her voice was unsteady. He could hear and feel her fear.

"Not sure, but not long. I was able to get a call to Caleb, so he's likely out there now. We can't open the door until we know he's there, and I have set my phone to silent."

She gave a little laugh. "Good thinking. No use warning everyone where we're hidden."

A sound at the wall stopped them and they shrank as far back as they could. A hand on Blues' neck showed his hackles raised. A low growl rumbled from deep within him.

A crack of light showed and then widened as the panel opened. It blinded them. They could hear voices but for a minute couldn't make out the words.

Blues snarled and barked.

"Call off your dog, Joshua." Joshua's eyes slid closed in relief as he heard Caleb.

"Blues, down." Blues moved and then stopped growling. His tail brushed against the wall, giving whispers of sound.

"You can come out now. It's safe. It was kids. They thought Blues was a wild dog and starting shooting at him. Are you both okay?"

"We are." Joshua took Laycee's hand and led her out of the room. They both stopped to let their eyes adjust back to the sunlight and then looked around.

Laycee sprang towards her brothers, who enveloped her in a huge hugs. Shudders and suppressed sobs shook her. Liam's eyes raised, to stare first at Caleb and then Joshua.

"We need to get her away from her and somewhere safe." He felt like he was stating the obvious.

—

"No, Liam." Laycee pulled back. "I'm not running. I can't. I have to work Tuesday and there is no way I'm not."

"Laycee, it's not safe. We don't know yet who's after you or why."

Laycee stood back from her brothers, hands on hips, and glared at them. "Stop plying the oldest brother card, Liam. It won't work. You know right well I have to work. Being the only secretary means that I do."

The three siblings debated this, at times with voices raised. Caleb looked at Joshua, who just shrugged, a smile on his face. Caleb shook his head and then turned to the door when Ben appeared, beckoning him outside.

Caleb and Ben walked towards the water and then stopped.

"What do you have?"

"Something interesting. I don't know how it connects, but one of those boys is the son of an accountant in town."

Caleb shared a look with Ben, then turned to where the youths were standing, handcuffed and waiting to be taken into town. "We need to process them. We're not letting them off. But we need to make sure that no one but you and I know the connection to Laycee. This is just getting too bizarre for words." Caleb rubbed the back of his neck, lost in thought. How much deeper was it going to get? "Take them into town and start processing them. They're over 18 so we don't need to call their parents.

Make sure to do everything by the book, and I mean everything."

Ben nodded, then glanced at the cabin. "They're ok? It sounded like it."

"Yeah. So far. We need to meet somewhere and come up with a plan to end this. It's getting to the point that something bad is going to happen and we won't be able to prevent it because we haven't a clue. Call me when you're done with those over there. I'll try and figure out what and where."

Ben took a step away and then turned. "Marg said she was getting together with Hannah and some ladies from the church to go over to Laycee's house and try and clean it up for her. Is that safe?"

Caleb's gaze met Ben's. "I guess it's as safe as anywhere. But hold her off for a few hours. I want Laycee to walk back through her house and see if anything is missing. Knowing her, she'll know as soon as she walks in."

Ben shook his head. "More than likely." With a wave, he strode over to the youths and all had soon disappeared down the lane.

—

Chapter 13

Caleb stepped back into the cabin

"Still at it, are they?" He asked Joshua.

Joshua laughed. "You got it. I think Laycee is winning."

Caleb smiled. "I think you're right. Those two are just so happy she's safe, I think they'll let her." He paused. "Laycee needs to go back to her house." As Joshua started to shake his head, Caleb continued, "She needs to see if anything is missing. No one else knows what she has in her house, only she does. She's determined to go back to work on Tuesday and it will take the next couple of days to get everything sorted around. You can bet those two won't let her stay on her own."

Joshua's gaze went to Laycee. She was becoming so important to him now and he didn't think he could handle anything else happening. "Yeah, you're right. Are we done here now?"

Caleb nodded, then strode over to where the three Bradley siblings were still locked in a heated battle of words.

"Okay, you three. Enough!" The firmness of his voice cut through the words and all three turned in surprise to stare at him. "We're done here. Laycee, we need you to go back through your house and see if anything is missing. Let me have the original of that document, show me where it was found, and then we're gone."

Laycee complied. Walking back down the lane in single file, Laycee kept very close to Joshua, with Blues tight to her side.

"You can have your dog back, Joshua. I'm going to find mine."

Joshua laughed. "Not happening. I think he's adopted you. You're part of his family now."

They sorted out themselves into vehicles. Laycee refused to go with either one of her brothers, causing raised eyebrows and questioning looks. She just stuck her nose up in the air and climbed into the vehicle with Joshua.

No words were exchanged on the drive to her house. They weren't needed. Joshua reached for Laycee's hand and held it. She looked at their hands, looked at him, gave a small smile, and then stared out the window. He was becoming important to her and she wasn't sure how she felt or if she even wanted him to be.

Joshua pulled into her driveway and parked. Stopping her from getting out, he caught her eyes.

"Let Caleb go through the house again. Let him make sure it's okay. You don't have to do this on your own. We're here for you."

Laycee swallowed hard, emotions mixed, but anger and fear predominant. Who had been in her house? And why? She was a secretary, not into crime, and she felt confident that her boss, a prominent physician, was the same. Now what? She knew she had to go in but she was just so hesitant.

She stepped out of the vehicle and stood watching as Caleb entered. Leith jogged over and draped his arm around her shoulders.

"Cheer up, hun. Caleb will make sure it's okay for you to go in. You know that."

Laycee laid her head on her brother's shoulder and drew in a shaky breath. When she left late yesterday afternoon (and was it not even 24 hours?) she didn't know she would be returning home to this. She never imagined she would be running for her life.

Liam's gaze wandered all over the neighbourhood, taking in vehicles parked on the street. He stopped by Laycee and asked, "Do you see any vehicles that don't belong?"

She looked around and shook her head.

Caleb appeared on her front porch and beckoned them forward. Laycee hesitated. She was not ready to do this. She was not ready to see what destruction was there.

Caleb came down the steps and stopped in front of her, bending so he could look into her downcast eyes. "It's not nice, Laycee. I won't lie to you. There doesn't look to be a lot of damage, just stuff tossed around."

Laycee looked up at him and nodded. Liam and Leith each took a hand and the three walked forward. Caleb glanced at Joshua, and then his gaze stopped at the look on his brother's face. He nodded. Yep, he thought, he has it bad and I can remember that feeling.

Caleb came up behind them. "I'm sorry, Laycee. I know it's a mess from the crime tech crew.

We'll get it cleaned up for you." He stopped and pulled out his phone. It was Ben and it looked as if he was needed back at the office. He took his leave, promising to have Hannah come by to help Laycee clean.

Laycee took a deep breath and stepped into her home. Tears filled her eyes as she looked at the destruction in her living room. Pictures were off the wall, frames and glass broken. Pillows and seat cushions from her couch and chairs were slashed and the stuff spread around. The few knick knacks she allowed herself were in pieces. She walked through into the dining room and then the kitchen. The kitchen was the worse, with everything from her cupboard pulled out and broken and spilt. The same went for the fridge. She turned and headed down the hall to the bedrooms. It was the same.

She sank to the floor and cradled her head on her knees as sobs wracked her body. She had been through so much in the last few hours. When would it end?

An arm came around her shoulders and a head was laid on hers. She knew it was Joshua. He said nothing, simply sat and held her until the sobs stopped. She could hear her brothers gathering up the broken glass and broken pieces of her life. She raised her head and stared ahead.

Joshua saw the change that came across her face. It was not a nice change. She was deeply angry and ready to fight back, but he was afraid for her. He didn't know if she would win or lose and he didn't want to take the chance that she would be gone from his life. He gently brushed back her hair and tried to get her to look at him.

Laycee shook off Joshua's arm and sprang to her feet. She was mad and you didn't make a Bradley mad. Her anger she would work off in cleaning and tidying up her home but it would also be directed at finding the culprits.

Later that afternoon, when her house was back to as normal as it could be and the broken and destroyed furniture removed, Laycee wandered through her house. Leith had gone to get her pets at her insistence. She needed them.

Now, she needed her laptop. It was gone. She looked around and made sure. Then as the two men watched, she stomped across the dining room to the built-in cabinet and pulled out an ornamental leaf. A section moved and a safe appeared. She punched in the code and pulled out a black box.

"What's that?" Liam asked.

"It's my backup. I always store everything to an external hard drive—there is nothing stored on the laptop so when they took it they got nothing. Though why they would think there is something on it I don't know. I don't have work stuff on it. Nothing. It's like a brand-new computer. It also has a really good password, one that would be really hard to break."

Chapter 14

Ben looked up as Caleb walked by him and then at his nod followed him into his office, closing the door behind him. Both men sat. Caleb took a sip of the tea he had picked up on his way in. It was getting late and he needed to get home.

"What do you have?"

"Something interesting. Those young fellows are mixed up in something big. They're scared right now and not saying much. They haven't asked for lawyers yet so I'm hoping a night in jail will make them talk." Ben thought for a minute. "One of them is related to the accountant. I think we need to do some more research on them. I am still trying to figure out the Applewood Farm connection."

"I agree. Who's good at research that we can bring on board, who we can absolutely trust? I don't want too many involved as yet, but I know talk is going to get around about what happened today. Were we able to keep it quiet about why Laycee was there?"

"I think so. As far as it goes, Laycee was there with Joshua for a day away from town. That's what I've put out. I don't like not telling the truth but in this case we need to protect Laycee. Try Annie - she's really good at sourcing information."

"Most definitely. All right, Ben, wrap it up for the day and head home. I'm going soon."

"See you tomorrow. Make sure you get some down time. I am pretty sure it's going to get very interesting very soon."

"You know, I hate it when you're right."

Ben laughed, closing the door behind him. Caleb worked for a while longer and then headed home to his wife and boys. He needed to be with them.

****

Laycee dug her fingers into Defiant's fur as he lay curled up tight to her on the couch Liam had brought over for her. Her couch and some other furniture would need to be replaced as would picture frames. She was tired just thinking about it. It helped to have Defiant next to her. He had gone wild when Leith brought him back late that afternoon, barking, jumping, doing his Sheltie spins and dances. When she sank to the floor, he had been all over her— kisses, on her knee, away and then back for her hugs. Terror, when let out of her crate, had taken one look, nose in the air, and then meandered over to the laundry room where Laycee kept her food dish up on the dryer. When she had inspected her domain, she returned and rubbed up against her, back arched and her tail doing its quiver that she gave when she was content and eager to please.

Laycee's head went back on the couch and her eyes sank closed. She was tired and needed some sleep. Liam had insisted he was staying the night and at the moment, was out on her back deck. She knew he had a cup of coffee with him—he never seemed to be without one. She hated that he and Leith and Joshua had gotten so involved in what was happening, whatever that was. She had sent Leith and Joshua home about an hour ago.

Liam came in, shutting and locking the back door, and setting her alarm.

"We need to look at better locks for you."

Laycee snorted. "Like that will help? They managed to disarm the alarm system by cutting the cable and then breaking in. I don't think better locks will make any difference."

"Maybe not."

Laycee rose, cutting off his next words. She had a pretty good idea of what was coming and was in no mood to listen. "I'm heading for bed. See you in the morning."

Liam stopped her with a hand to her arm. "I'm glad you're okay. God was watching out for you. I just want you around for a few more years."

Laycee dropped a quick kiss on his forehead. "I know. I've got a few years of bugging you left to do."

Liam laughed. "Night, hun."

****

Tom was running scared. Somehow he had heard what had happened at the Bradley cottage. Word had gotten around among some of his friends. He had no idea where Andy was but he could only hope Andy was not one of the punks who had shot up the cottage, aiming at a dog. It would be like him to have that happen.

The trilling of his phone startled him. He took a quick look. It was the Boss. He threw his phone across the room, breaking it. He was done. He grabbed a duffel bag from the closet and stuffed it full of his and Andy's clothing. That was all that they had that was theirs in this rundown trailer. He was out of here. He would try and find Andy and barring that, he was out of town tonight. He had no idea where he was headed but it was far from here.

He didn't bother locking the door—there was nothing to steal. He jumped in his vehicle, keyed it to life and burnt rubber as he left the park. After driving around for a while, he headed out of town. No, Andy was underground somewhere or else he had messed up and was in jail. He would try and find him once he got settled in a new town. Maybe he should just get a job and stay away from crime. Crime certainly wasn't working for him right now.

****

The Boss cursed. That no-good punk was not answering his phone. He slammed his glass down on the desk, spilling his drink. His employer was coming down on him to find the information and he had had to hire two low-downs to try and find it. They messed up, which meant he had messed up. Mistakes were not permissible. His life was now on the line and he intended to make Laycee pay when he got his hands on her and got the information he needed.

His phone rang, stilling his inner raging. It was her, the Mastermind. He didn't know what he was going to say, how he was going to explain that he no longer had control of the two he had hired and that he was no closer to finding what she wanted. She wouldn't take it well. Failure was not an option. It was life or death for him, his life or his death. He had

———

money squirrelled away in banks overseas that no one knew about. He intended to live and live well once he got out of the country.

Chapter 15

The Sunday morning sun peeked over the horizon. Laycee's eyes opened. She knew sleep was over, and it was only 5 a.m. She reached over and hugged Defiant, sleeping tight to her, and then reached for Terror, sleeping perched on her as she lay on her side. Terror's purrs started and she licked Laycee's arm.

Laycee shoved Defiant enough that he jumped off the bed, followed by Terror. The two were inseparable, not typical for cat and dog. Laycee grabbed her mint green terrycloth robe and shoved her arms into it. She headed for the back door to let the dog out and then reached for the animals' food dishes for their breakfast. She filled their water bowls, one in the kitchen, the other in the living room. Stretching, she looked around her house. It looked empty but the sunny yellow of the walls, the dark laminate flooring and the cream trim and ceiling always perked her spirits. Today it didn't. She still felt violated at the intrusion into her home. She lifted her heart to God, asking for protection and peace.

When she turned back to the kitchen, Liam was standing at her island. She loved that kitchen—the off-white cabinets, solid brown countertop and polished bronze fixtures. A little oak island in the middle was all she needed. The kitchen wasn't big enough for a table but she had a dining room; that's all she needed.

"So," Liam asked. "How are you? And what mischief do you plan on getting into today?"

Laycee swatted him on the way by. "I'm fine, and the mischief was not of my making." Nose in the air, she made her way to the fridge, then realized she didn't have much in the way of groceries to make breakfast, thanks to the intruders yesterday.

"Go, get yourself ready. We'll go out for breakfast. It's almost 7 now. Deb will have the cafe open."

"If it's your treat?"

"It is. Get going. I'll make sure the animals are taken care of."

Laycee stepped out of her house and looked around. It seemed normal, but she was nervous. She felt like there were eyes boring into her back, watching every move she was taking away from her safe spot. She quickly jumped into Liam's vehicle.

"Laycee, Caleb is meeting us. He called when you were getting ready. Just us three. He needs to run something by you."

Laycee turned her head to look at her brother, shrugged, and then turned her gaze back out the window. She didn't notice that Liam's eyes kept going to the rearview mirror. He thought they were being followed but wasn't sure. He wasn't the police, so he really didn't know how to tell.

Caleb was waiting for them in a back booth at the Crazy Quilt Cafe. Deb Saunders, the owner, loved quilting almost as much as she loved to cook and had decided this was the perfect name for her place. Liam let Laycee slide onto the black vinyl bench seat and then slid in beside her.

Caleb waited until they had placed their orders and then looked at Laycee.

"Laycee, we have some things to go over. I have some questions to ask as well." He stopped speaking as their food was placed in front of them and Liam offered a quick prayer of thanks.

"Caleb, I would rather not answer anything right now, not here." Laycee gaze shot around the cafe. She felt eyes on her but who? Everyone in the cafe at that point she knew from town. It was not a large town, small town in fact, but right now, she wished to be in a huge city where anonymity was the norm.

Caleb nodded. "That we can do. Somewhere else. So tell me, Liam, how's work?"

Liam's fork stopped halfway to his mouth and then he laughed. "Quick change of subject, there, my friend. Work is going well. How are your gardens?"

The two men's conversation drifted off into mundane, every day topics. Caleb dropped money on the table for their meal and then stood.

Laycee and Liam followed him from the cafe.

Caleb stood by his personal truck, eyes searching the area. He too felt uncomfortable, a sense of danger, and he had learned to never ignore his gut feelings. "Okay. Let's take my vehicle. We need to talk and it's probably the best not to talk in public."

Once they were seated in Caleb's truck, he hesitated. "We need to go back over the whole timeline again." At Laycee's startled look, he continued, "We don't have your statement. I want you to walk me back over everything that you can remember. Here, dictate into this and I can have it transcribed for you to sign." He handed her a small dictator.

She looked at it and then him. "Dark ages still, Caleb?"

He shrugged and then laughed. "It works."

Laycee directed him to the restaurant where it all started on Friday night, going over each step she had taken, who she could remember seeing there, to the point where she had fled. He drove to where her truck had gone off the road. She shuddered as she looked at the area, knowing it was only God's hand that kept her from serious injury.

He then drove to the Bradley cabin and parked in front of it. He turned off the vehicle, then laid a hand on her arm.

"We're going to go in, Laycee. We need to search this place as well to see if there is anything else here. Someone was in here and left that envelop. There may have been more than one occasion that happened."

Laycee shuddered at the thought. "Did you ever figure out what the paper said?"

Caleb was silent long enough that Laycee turned to look at him. He nodded. "I am not going to tell you until after your statement is finished and signed."

They searched the cabin. Nothing was found. Laycee looked around, then stepped outside, a thoughtful look on her face. Where would someone hide something?

Liam came up behind her. "Still thinking?"

"Yeah. Where would you hide something if you wanted to make sure no one else found it?"

Brother and sister looked at the out buildings, and then at each other. Both raced for the boat house. Caleb followed them, knowing they were on to something, or at least he hoped they were.

Liam reached up under the eaves above the entrance door. He felt something.

"Caleb, I think you need to pull this out. I don't think it's something we left from years ago."

Caleb took Liam's place and reached up to the small area. He felt a small paper package. He sighed. Sunday or not, his crime evidences team would be back. He knew they had searched the boathouse the day before but whether they had looked up at the eaves or not was another matter. Or else someone had been here since and placed this. He pulled out his phone, called for the team, and then hesitated. Phone slipped back into his jacket pocket, he turned to Liam and Laycee

"We might as well get comfortable in the cabin. Do you have any tea, Laycee?"

Laycee gave a small smile. "We do. A real variety. Which do you prefer?"

As Laycee and Caleb walked ahead of him, discussing the merits of various teas, Liam followed more slowly, deep in thought. This was getting out of hand. Who and what and why? His mind drifted to

—

the Applewood Farm B&B. A thought made him turn and look across the small lake. It was what he thought. The B&B was directly across the lake. Now it was making sense. He quickened his steps to catch up with the others and let Caleb know what he had discovered. Caleb took a step back and looked across the lake, then looked at Liam and nodded. Yes - things were beginning to make sense, but what kind of sense?

Chapter 16

The Mastermind was very angry. Someone had failed. Someone had messed up weeks and months of careful planning. It had come down to one person who had chosen wrongly. She stomped around her office, footsteps deadened by the plush cream carpet. Her gaze shot around the room but didn't take in the beautiful wood furniture, the dark wainscoting and trim, the maroon velvet drapes at the windows, or the cream wallpaper. She strode back to her desk and dropped into the luxurious desk chair. No expense had been spared in her office, although the rest of the house was not decorated to the degree this was.

She stabbed the number for the Boss. He was not answering. Her anger level continued to climb. Someone was going to pay for this. And that would start with that little brat, Laycee Bradley. It was her fault. Somehow, she had to have found out what was going on.

A knock at the door startled her. She was a master at concealing her emotions and quickly pulled a bland face over the anger.

"Come in."

Her housekeeper entered, handing her the morning mail, and then left.

The Mastermind flipped through the mail and stopped at an envelope that had just her name on it, not that of her organization. The return address was from Oak City, just the street address, no name.

Picking up her letter opener, she quickly slit open the envelope and withdrew the typed page. Her features darkened again in anger. How dare he? How dare he threaten to take away what she had accumulated? He would pay. Just as soon as she finished here.

****

Caleb watched his team pack up and leave. They had taken the package with them and would open it in the lab. A call would come to him once that was done. He scrubbed his hands down his face and then through his hair. It was going to be a long day. It was Sunday and he had planned to be at church with Hannah and their boys. He pulled out his phone and gave her a quick call, letting her know he might not make it.

Liam approached him, uncertainty in his steps and gaze. Caleb sighed. Whatever was going on just got a whole lot bigger and he still had to figure out how Laycee was involved.

A sound of an approaching vehicle caught his attention. It stopped and both Joshua and Leith stepped out. Liam must have called Leith. Now that the whole gang was here, maybe they could get some answers.

"Liam, why don't you see if you and Laycee can rustle up some coffee and tea and maybe something to eat? It's been a while since our breakfast and I could use something to fuel the brain cells."

Liam grinned. "That's all you think of, isn't it? You haven't changed. Sure, I'll get right on it."

—

Caleb smiled, shaking his finger at his friend. They had been in the same class at high school, but it was just over the last few years that their friendship had grown close. They were in a small men's Bible study group and often met for a quick coffee or lunch when they could swing it.

Joshua headed for the cabin as Leith approached Caleb. Leith's face was grim, making him seem so much older.

"What's going on, Caleb? We saw the team leaving."

Caleb hesitated, then indicated the cabin. "Let's go inside. We need to talk. I had the team sweep for bugs, so I know the place is clean."

"Bugs - as in…" Leith's voice trailed off.

Caleb nodded as they headed for the cabin. Laycee had made both coffee and tea and had mugs poured for all. She hadn't found much to prepare to eat but had found some soup and crackers that were still fresh.

Gathering around the table, Caleb took a sip of his tea and then, setting the mug back down, wrapped his hands around it. He closed his eyes and offered a quick prayer for wisdom and guidance. Looking around he searched the faces of the other four.

Liam was simmering with anger. The big brother in him was frankly showing on his face. His knuckles were white as he gripped his mug.

Next to him, Leith's face had become unreadable. There was rage palpating from him, nevertheless. His eyes were fixed on Laycee and Caleb found them shuttered. Leith had always been one who was very open with his emotions. Not any more.

His brother was next. Joshua sat beside Laycee, his eyes glued to her. Caleb knew his brother well. Joshua was in love and the woman he loved was in danger. Anger was there but determination was as well. Joshua was going to solve this, no matter the cost.

Caleb's gaze travelled back over the three men before resting on Laycee. Her eyes were down, looking at her clasped hands. They were loosely clasped, not clenched as he thought they would be. There was a look of peace on her face, strangely not fear or anger. He tilted his head as he contemplated what was going on with her. A few hours earlier, she had been afraid and terrorized. Not any more.

Caleb looked down, then looked once more at Laycee. He pulled over the tablet of paper and pen she had left on the table. Laycee had turned on a radio and soft music played in the background. He caught the song that was plying and nodded. Now he knew why she was calm. She had turned it over to God and He had put peace in her.

Chapter 17

The Boss had gone into hiding. He knew the Mastermind was after him. He had failed and failed mightily. His life was now in danger. He had packed up what he could and abandoned his apartment. He was hoping that they had found the parcel he left at the cabin. He knew the hiding place of the Bradley siblings. He had heard them talking about it in the past, back when they were all kids plying around the lake. He had withdrawn as much money as he could, had his passport in his fake name, and was just waiting for dark to get away. He had had enough. It wasn't worth it any more. Tickets were booked on a flight out of the country for tonight. He hoped he made it to the airport in Oak City.

Looking back, he regretted a lot. He didn't regret the wealth he had accumulated, but he did regret the danger he had put friends into.

A noise at the door of the abandoned house startled him. A shape appeared, a shot rang out, and he cried out in pain. As darkness closed in on him, he knew he had lost. He had played the game and the cards were no longer in his favour. He sank to the ground and the darkness overcame his sight. Empty hands stretched out. The form stood over him, then picked up his duffel bag. This is what his life had come to—dying in an abandoned house, alone, a victim of his own making.

****

The Mastermind grimaced at what she had had to do, but then smiled. One less person to worry about. She was taking control. She would be the one doing everything now. She had a source she could go to for information and that was what she intended to do. No one suspected who was in her pocket and deep in her pocket at that. She just needed to tidy up a few loose ends that the Boss had left. Time to search out those two losers he had hired. The boss may have once been from this area but he had been gone for years. No one would know he was missing. No one would know he was gone.

She turned and crept back through the woods. She hated the woods. She hated the bugs and animals. She hated the smell of the woods. She hated everything about them. Yet here she was stuck in one because the Boss messed up big time. He had paid. Now she would make the others pay for her discomfort.

****

Caleb cleared his throat; the three men's eyes shot to his face. He kept his eyes on Laycee. She seemed detached, lost in thought.

"Laycee." He began, then stopped as his phone rang. He stepped outside to take his call and then returned, looking down at a text he had just received. Yes, things were progressing, and this text just made something a little bit clearer.

Joshua reached over and gripped Laycee's hand. It was cold. She looked up at him from under her eyelashes and they shared a long look. She sighed and then looked at her brothers. She could

—

feel their emotions and wished she had never been the one to bring that to them, whatever "that" was.

Caleb seated himself again and hesitated before he spoke. "Laycee, I know we have gone over just about everything and that your statement is now ready to sign. However…" His voice trailed away as he sought for the words he needed to proceed. It was not going to be easy. It was actually going to be really difficult and he expected a fight from her.

"Laycee, that package was actually another note. We're working on finding out who the sender is, but it is someone who knows you and knows you fairly well. We need to be looking at your friends and those you have worked with, including those you volunteer with."

Laycee's eyes grew in size as he spoke, then slid close. It was what she had feared. Someone was after her. SHE had brought this danger to herself and her family and friends.

"Who and why?"

Caleb pulled up the text on his phone.

He read it silently to himself and then showed her:

Laycee

You are in danger. Someone wants you dead. You have something they want and unless you turn it over you won't be safe.

Turn it over and you just might live.

A Friend

Laycee gasped. What was going on? Who was doing this? As she grappled with this, Caleb shared the text with the other three. Glances were shared, plans were made with those glances, and Laycee's freedom to move around on her own just shrank.

"Do you have any idea?"

She shook her head. "I don't. I know just about everyone in town, mostly because of my job, and I can't say anything about that because of confidentiality. I can't think of anyone who stands out."

Caleb nodded. It was what he had suspected. Laycee was trusting and giving. She was loved by those she worked with and by her friends. Ben had checked and she was one of the volunteers the residents of the home looked forward to seeing the most. It would be difficult to determine who the person was, but he would do it. Joshua's face said the same.

Joshua abruptly shoved back his chair and lifted Laycee to her feet. "We're out of here. We'll meet you at your office." Clasping her hand he led her from the cabin, shoved her into his truck, and drove away.

The three remaining stared at the door, then at each other.

"He's got it bad." Leith snickered, bringing some levity to the moment.

"Yes, he has." Liam agreed. "Let's get this cleaned up. Caleb, we can manage. Head back into Riverville. Leith and I will do some brainstorming. You don't need all of us there. Just keep us as updated as you can."

"Will do. Thanks, guys. I hope and pray this is over in the next day or so, but I am thinking it won't be."

Laycee was silent as they drove back to Riverville, silent as Joshua stopped and got her a coffee from her favourite coffee shop, silent as he pulled up and parked at the police station, silent as they entered and waited to be cleared to go through, silent as he led her to Caleb's office, silent as she sat. He was getting worried. She was shutting him out and he didn't like it.

Caleb entered, Ben behind him, and shut the door. He didn't go behind his desk, instead perched on the edge near Laycee.

"Laycee, we have your statement here. We just need to have you proofread it and sign it that it's correct. Then we need to talk."

Laycee nodded woodenly, taking the file and pen she was handed. She quickly read her statement and then scrawled her signature.

She stood, hesitated and then headed for the door and was gone before anyone could stop her. This had surprised them. Joshua ran after her but she was already gone. He headed out the door and there was no sign of her. Caleb and Ben were at his heels. Caleb had suspected this. There were not a lot of places she could go to and he would look at each one. He sent a quick message to Liam.

Liam and Leith headed for Laycee's, knowing she would want her Sheltie and cat. They were her comfort.

Laycee had not shown up. Liam searched outside as Leith searched inside. He let Defiant out of his crate and into the backyard. Defiant followed Liam everywhere as he took in every aspect of the yard. Things seemed normal. Leith exited the back door, shaking his head at Liam's questioning look. Where was she?

Joshua's heart raced. Laycee had to be close. He frantically searched around his vehicle, around the station and then the surrounding blocks. She had totally disappeared. He asked anyone he came across. Laycee had not been seen.

Caleb sent Ben back in to alert the patrol officers to watch for Laycee. He had a bad feeling. She had moved so quick, they had not had time to react. Now they were behind and had to pick up the pieces and find her.

Chapter 18

Hours later, they regrouped at Laycee's house. Leith carried Terror around; she needed that contact.

Caleb looked up from the papers he had in his hand. "No sign of her. Either she's very good at hiding or someone has her. I'm afraid my gut says it's the latter."

They nodded. A command centre had now been set up in Laycee's dining room. Liam slammed his fist on the wall and then left to the back yard. Defiant crept close to him as he sat down on the steps. Hugging his sister's dog, he bowed his head and prayed. A fervent prayer that his sister would be found.

It was a long night. No word. No sleep. By morning, they just knew something was wrong.

Liam's phone vibrated. He pulled it out and stared at it. Laycee had sent a text.

"I'm fine. Had to think. Home soon. Feed Defiance and Kat for me." He stilled.

"Caleb, look at this." He handed him his phone.

"She's fine and on her way home?"

Leith and Joshua stood staring at them. All this for nothing?

Liam shook his head. "It's not her. She would never mix up the name of her dog and she never calls Terror Kat."

Caleb looked grim. Issuing orders, steps were set in process to track her phone.

Officers had spoken to Laycee's employer, her friends, the therapy pet organization, nurses and staff at the seniors' home. Nothing stood out. But there was something there, something off, that Caleb couldn't put his finger on.

An officer entered and spoke quietly with Caleb. He searched the room and beckoned Ben over. They spoke for a few minutes and then Ben left.

Caleb approached Liam and Leith. "No word yet. Ben had to leave for something else. We'll find her."

Liam's grim gaze met Caleb, a challenge in the eyes. "So far, we haven't. Each moment it takes makes it more dangerous for her."

Leith stood shoulder to shoulder with Liam, united in their search.

"Look. I need to leave for a while. I'll be back. Officers are speaking with her neighbours again. There were some who were away over the weekend. I take it you'll both be staying here?" At their nods, he turned and left.

****

Joshua sat at his kitchen island, absently rubbing the soft golden fur around Blues' ears. Chin on Joshua's leg, Blues sighed in contentment and closed his eyes. Joshua took a swig of water and then pulled his tablet over. Touching it, he brought up a word processing program and starting listing: dates, events, friends he had, friends Laycee had, groups she was part of that he knew about. There was just too much information.

He rose and moved into the living room, parting the drapes to look out. A cruiser sat in front of his house; Caleb was being thorough. Joshua let the drapes fall back into place and turned. He knew how to do renovations, not how to plan a crime and institute it or to take it apart and understand the mentality behind it. He stopped, an idea crossing his mind. He needed his computer, not his tablet this time. He booted up the computer and started. It made sense to think through this by first deconstructing what had happened and then following the pieces.

Hours later, he rubbed his eyes. He was tired, his eyes closing on him. He thought he had something and looked at the clock. He couldn't call anyone at 3 a.m. He would have to wait. He saved what he was working on and headed for bed. He needed some sleep. Maybe it would be clearer to his muddled mind in the morning.

A couple of hours later, Joshua stirred. Blues was up and moving around, unusual for him at night. Joshua quickly dressed and crept down his stairs. Blues was at the back door, woofing quietly. Joshua peeked through the blinds and saw nothing. He unlocked the door and let Blues out. The dog streaked for the back of the yard, quiet barks floating back. The barks stopped abruptly. Joshua stepped out on the deck, calling for Blues. He stepped down the few steps and onto the flag stones. He moved toward the back of the yard, intent on finding Blues. A whisper of a sound came too late. He felt a crushing blow and then blackness overcame him. He

—

didn't feel the hands that picked him up roughly and slung him over a shoulder, didn't feel the pain of being thrown into the back seat of a pickup, didn't feel the jouncing. Hands dragged him out of the truck eventually, carried him to a building and then let him fall to the cold damp dirt. He didn't hear the clicking of a padlock nor feel the silence and darkness around him.

****

Leith and Liam stretched out on the blankets on the Laycee's living room floor. Defiant curled up tight to Liam, and Terror had plopped herself atop Leith. They needed to be comforted as well as give comfort.

"Where do you think she is?" Leith's voice was quiet and sad.

There was silence, then "I wish I knew. She disappeared so fast. Joshua said he was out the door in just minutes and she was gone. She had no vehicle; she had to get a ride with someone."

"Sure but why isn't she here? She would be even if she had gotten a ride."

"I know. Mom would say pray about it and leave it with God. He's in control and cares more about us than anything. I just wish she and Dad were here right now to pray."

Leith nodded, even though Liam couldn't see him. The silence grew, soon broken by the men's soft snores. Terror rose, stretched and jumped off Leith, making her way to the front window and ducking in behind the drapes. Plopping herself down on the windowsill, she watched the car sitting in front of the house, no lights, no movement from it. Unblinking, she watched, head moving to follow it as it pulled away. Taillights didn't appear until it was around the corner. Who was watching, she would have asked if she was human. She lifted her paw and started washing the black and white fur, interest lost in the outdoors.

Leith started at the sound of a door closing. He jumped and looked around him. Then he remembered where he was. Liam was still sound asleep, Defiant still curled up tight to him, but brown eyes open and watchful.

Leith rose and moved to the window. Opening the drapes, he saw Caleb making his way to the door. Checking his watch, he was surprised that it was after 8. They must have been tired. He would soon need to drop by his office to see if the material had arrived and he knew Liam needed to get to his job site. He walked over and gave Liam a nudge with his foot. "Caleb's here. Come on, sunshine. Time to rise and shine."

Liam grunted and then sat up as Leith opened the door. Caleb handed him a takeout tray of coffee, snagging his own cup of tea, and the bag of biscuits and bagels he had picked up.

"Any word?" Liam asked.

Caleb grunted, then motioned with the bag. "First, we eat. Then we talk. It's gonna be a long day."

Caleb was right. It was a long day that worked its way to another and another. They were growing tired, with little sleep and little food and little news.

Caleb had had an officer stationed outside during the night until he had been needed in another area of town.

Chapter 19

"Ben!" Caleb yelled for him as he headed for the door and his vehicle.

Ben looked up and then followed. "What's up?"

"A couple of hunters were out checking out their blinds and cabins, to see what repairs they needed to make before fall. I know, it's only September but you know Earl and Henry. They like everything in order. Apparently they stumbled upon a body in an abandoned cabin near Logan Lake."

Ben froze, then looked over. "Joshua!"

Caleb shrugged. "It doesn't fit the description of what he was wearing and the responding officer said the man's build was wrong. I want you to take a look at this and see if it fits in with Laycee's case." He slammed his open hand on the steering wheel. "I just wish I knew where those two were."

"I know, I know." Ben agreed. "I've working on the lists with Liam and Leith. We've been able to eliminate quite a few people. There are some names we're not sure of, so I'm doing further checking."

"Let's meet later today and go over everything then. Maybe we'll have an ID on the body by then."

Caleb pulled to a stop near the coroner's van and got out. He headed over to the detective who was heading up the investigation.

———

Jim Townsend looked up at Caleb and shook his head. Caleb's eyes shut in relief. It wasn't Joshua.

"Who do we have?"

"I have no idea why he would be out here or why he was shot, but it's Peter Adams."

Caleb and Ben shot a look at each other. "Peter Adams. Now that rings a bell. Wasn't he the forger we were looking for, last from Oak City?"

"That he was. I gather that's who you've found?"

Jim nodded. "It looks as if he's been here for four days or so. The coroner will know more once he's done the autopsy. He still had his wallet and all his ID. Looks like one bullet to the head."

"Execution style. That just adds a whole new case to our overloaded books. We're going to be looking for who hired him."

Jim looked at Caleb, hesitated, and then said, "He's around the same age as Laycee and Joshua. In fact, I think I saw he was in Laycee's high school class."

Caleb shot Jim a look. What would a forger have in common with Laycee?

****

Joshua roused, prying open his eyes. Blackness swirled in front of him and his eyelids slid closed. Later, he opened his eyes again, and the world stood still. He moved cautiously rolling over onto his back. He felt lightheaded but there was no more blackness. He turned his head, taking in where he was. It was an old boat house, he thought, as he could hear water nearby. He sat up and regretted it as the world spun and nausea rose. Fighting back against both, he stumbled to his feet swaying for a minute. He shivered, feeling the dampness and the coldness, yet burning up at the same time. He focused on the door and inched his way over, his head pounding with each step. He pulled on the door and yanked it open. Sudden sunlight tortured him. His eyes closed, he dropped to his knees and then fell forward, blackness once again closing in.

The sudden noise of a door being pulled open stopped the officers at the cabin. Ben spun, looked at Caleb, and then drew his weapon as he headed for the noise. Caleb, weapon in hand, followed as did some of the other officers. They halted at the edge of a clearing, ensuring it was safe.

"Caleb. Over there at the boat house? Is that a body?"

Caleb squinted against the bright sun and nodded. They cautiously made their way across the small clearing, trusting in the officers behind them to keep them safe. They stopped just short of the boat house and looked around.

Caleb squatted down and reached for the body. He felt the movement of the back and knew the man was alive. He holstered his weapon and turned the man over.

"Joshua!" he cried. He could hear Ben in the background yelling to get an ambulance. He quickly felt over Joshua's body for wounds, stopping at the back of his head. There was a nasty lump there. Caleb knew he had to leave his brother lay still until the paramedics had assessed him and could move him safely. "Ben, get blankets. We need to get him warm."

Ben raced for the vehicles and returned as quickly as he could. Tucking the blankets around Joshua, he laid a hand on Caleb's shoulders and then moved away. He stepped into the boat house and looked around. It was empty, except for some skittering of little feet and cobwebs. He shuddered, thinking of how Joshua had laid there for overnight.

Caleb watched as the paramedics worked on his brother and then moved him to a stretcher. He followed behind. Ben stopped him with a hand on his arm.

"Call Hannah. Then go with him. I'll process this and catch up with you. Davis will drive you." He motioned to one of the young officers standing nearby. "Drive Caleb to this hospital and then go get his wife, Hannah."

Davis nodded and reached for Caleb's keys. Caleb handed them over almost without thought.

Hannah raced into the Emergency Department, frantically searching for her husband among the people waiting. She saw him as he turned and slammed her body into his.

"It's really Joshua?" she asked. At his nod, she continued, "How is he?"

"Dr. Young is with him now. They're running tests and he said something about an X-Ray or a CT of the head. Joshua was knocked out and it looks like he was unconscious for a time. They need to make sure there is no damage. We have to wait until we speak with him to find out how long he was out there." Caleb's voice broke.

Hannah drew him over to a chair and pulled him down with her. She looked up as their pastor and his wife approached. "Sweetheart, Pastor Bob and Sue are here. Let's pray."

Gathering around them, the pastor led them in prayer, bringing Joshua to the Lord for healing and also for Laycee to be found. The room silenced around them, hushed at the solemnity and seriousness of the moment.

Dr. Young emerged from the exam rooms and looked for Caleb. Hannah touched his arm and pointed. Caleb rose as the physician approached.

"Good news, Caleb. Good news. Looks like a concussion but nothing more serious. He's been in the elements, though, and we'll need to keep him for a day or so to make sure nothing comes of that."

Caleb's eyes slid shut and then reopened. He shook the physician's hand and thanked him.

As he turned, he say Liam and Leith hovering near the door. He spoke to Hannah and then preached them.

"We heard," Liam said. "Is he okay?"

Caleb nodded. "Concussion. Exposure but Dr. Young thinks he's okay."

Leith's hands clenched into fists. "Any idea of why or who?"

Caleb shook his head. "Too soon. Ben's working the area and will let me know what he finds.

As soon as I can, I'm headed back to talk with Joshua."

"My gut says it's related to Laycee. I spoke with Ben. He said you found the body of a forger in the woods nearby. Any relation to this?"

Caleb was silent, trying to come up with the words that would dispel their fear and worry without being overheard in a room full of listeners.

He nodded to the outside door and they stepped through it.

"I think somehow it is. It is starting to make sense. I need to speak with the police department in Oak City to see what they have and then track his steps. I want Laycee found too."

"We know you do." Leith's voice was taut with worry. It had been four days since Laycee was seen and he felt they were no closer to finding her or what had happened to her. "I need to go. I'll talk to you later." He spun on his heel and rushed away.

They watched him go. Liam's voice reached to Caleb, "He's worried and he wants to help, just doesn't know how. What can I do?"

"You're not a police officer, Liam, but I could use your help. I want to stay and see Joshua as soon as he's back in a room. Then let's meet. Hopefully Ben will be back in town and has some answers."

Liam nodded and watched as his friend trudged back through the doors. This was wearing everyone down, but Caleb seemed to be hit the worst at the moment. Finding his brother alive would help but they still needed answers. He raised his eyes to the sky and sent up a silent prayer, once again pleading for his sister.

****

Five hours later, the four men sat around the kitchen table in Caleb's home. Papers and files were stacked on the table. Hannah moved around, making sure they had their food and drinks and then, dropping a kiss on Caleb's cheek, left the room to spend time with her sons.

"Ben, let's start with prayer. Humanly, we're doing everything I think we can. We could sure use some divine intervention right now."

Ben led them in prayer, pleading for Laycee, asking for healing for Joshua, and for wisdom and strength for themselves. He reminded the Lord that they were the apple of His eye and that He cared for sparrows, much more so for them.

There was silence, then paper rustling as Caleb sorted through what he had and what he could share with the two Bradley men. He had spoken to the mayor and the police board and knew they were on board with them being involved. Being upright and honest men in the community helped.

The silence continued as they read their material. Liam, always needs a visual thanks to his landscaping skills, reached for a tablet of paper and a pen to start charting ideas.

———

Chapter 20

Caleb rose and made fresh tea for himself and a pot of coffee for the others, refilling their mugs when it was brewed. He stretched and looked at the clock. It was late.

He studied the other three and paced through the house and up the stairs. Stopping at his boys' room, he entered. They were sound asleep. He pulled the covers up more tightly on them and dropped a kiss on each of the heads.

He left and turned towards his own bedroom. Hannah was still up, curled up in a blanket in her favourite chair, a light on low, and her Bible on her knee. He crouched down beside her and she drew him into a hug.

"How's it going?" She asked.

"We're not getting far. I just know we're missing something but I don't know what." He sighed. "It would be nice if you can up with an idea. You always have great ideas."

"Well, thank you." She kissed him and then drew back. "I do have an idea but I didn't want to influence you."

He cocked his head and waited. He knew she was searching for words, something she would do when she wanted to explain something and wasn't sure how to proceed.

"You think it is something Laycee is involved in?" At his nod, she continued, "Okay. She has her friends, her church, her work, and her volunteer duties. You have pretty much eliminated her friends, her work and her church. That leaves her volunteer duties. About all I know she is involved with is the Take-A-Lick Pet Therapy. It's run by an accountant in town, Joy Smith. I don't think you'll find anything with the Applebys from Applewood Farm. I have known Doris and George for years. What you would likely find is that someone stayed there, contacted someone here and it went from there."

Caleb stared at her, amazed at how succinct an explanation she had just given. She was right. They had eliminated just about everything else.

"Hannah, you're wonderful. No wonder I love you so much." He kissed her, spun and raced out of the room.

Hannah touched her mouth and smiled. Yes, Caleb was now on a hunt. Thank the Lord that He had given her those thoughts tonight.

Caleb's phone rang as he descended the stairs. It was the hospital, letting him know that Joshua had been awake, talking but had drifted off to a normal sleep. That buoyed his steps even more.

The three men looked up as he sat back down. He looked around at them.

"Hannah, bless her, has had a suggestion. What do you know about Take-A-Lick Pet Therapy and its founder, Joy Smith?"

Ben's pen dropped. "That's it. That's what has been bugging me. Rumours are that Joy is in financial difficulty. You know she does a lot of freebie work at the seniors' home. Worth a looksee at her."

Liam and Leith's eyes snapped between the two officers. Were they finally getting somewhere?

"Okay, it's getting late. Let's pick it up in the morning. Ben, I want you to go through her financials. Get a court order if you have too. Get Lucy to take a look at the seniors' home, match up any deaths with the residents Laycee has recently visited."

"Leith, Liam, what do you know about Peter Adams?"

Leith's eyes met Liam, then shot to Caleb.

"Peter was in some of Laycee's classes. He tried hard to get her to go out with him, but she wouldn't. She would never tell us why, other than he wasn't her type. I always thought there was more."

Liam picked up the thread. "He's Joy Smith's son, you know. Dad had heard rumours that he was just a hair away from being in trouble with the law. Laycee said he could copy his Mom's signature and was always signing excuses to get out of school."

Ben and Caleb shared a glance. It was closing in on Joy Smith. They needed more information and proof.

****

The next morning, he was met in his office by the three men. Ben looked excited, so Caleb knew he had some information.

Leith spoke. "Mrs. Appleby called last night, asking about Laycee. We know them from the years at the lake. She said she hadn't seen Joy for a couple of years, that they had used her for their accounts, but in the last couple of years, she was really pushing them to invest in funds she controlled. They weren't comfortable with that and changed their accountant."

Ben was nodding. "That's what I've been hearing, too. She's pushing for investments. Some of the seniors at the home were approached and refused. Interestingly, there were about three or four who said no, but when the family checked their accounts after they died, it showed investment withdrawals. They weren't aware of this. I'm having Annie track these down."

Liam was silent. "So it's all about money? Is that why Laycee was chased and has now disappeared?"

"We don't know for sure, Liam, but I will have traces put on Joy's business and personal accounts and have an unmarked car follow her. We'll also find out if that forger from Oak City had contact with her. What I was hearing is that Joy and Peter were estranged. The police detective last involved in his case is investigating that now and will email his findings. He hoped to have something solid by noon."

Anger simmered just below the surface. Joshua had been injured and Laycee was missing. This drew them together closer than any blood ties.

A tap came at the door, and Annie appeared at Caleb's invitation to enter. She handed him a folder and before releasing it, sent him a look. He studied her and then nodded. Yes, she had come through. He wanted to go through the information first, then with Ben before he shared it any further.

After the men had left, Caleb headed over to the hospital to see Joshua. Entering his room, he found him sitting on the side of the bed, dressed.

"Where do you think you are going?"

Squinting at him, Joshua replied, "To find Laycee."

"No. You're hurt and you're not steady on your feet. I'm taking you to Hannah. Fill me in on what happened."

"I don't know. I remember sitting there, Blues wanting out, not getting Blues to come back. I stepped out and that's the last I remember. How long was I gone?"

Caleb figured it would be this way but still had had to ask. "Let's get you home. And you were gone for about 12-18 hours. Do you remember what you are doing last?"

Joshua sighed, his headache making thinking difficult and blurring his vision. "I was working on trying to sort out a timeline and people and had gone to bed. Blues alerted and I followed him outside. That's the last I remember. If I can get to my computer, I need to show you something. I think it's tied to the therapy group and seniors. At least that's what I thought."

Caleb nodded, helped Joshua to a wheelchair and pushed him outside. The sun caused Joshua to blink and cringe at the renewed headache. "I think you're on to something. That's what we've figured out too."

As Caleb drove towards his home (Joshua would be spending time with them), he continued, "Tell me what you know about Peter Adams?"

"Peter?" Joshua's brow crinkled in thought. "I haven't heard of him in years, since before I finished high school. He had left town about the time his Mom remarried. He didn't like the guy. He wouldn't even come back after Joy divorced him. I don't think Joy and Peter got along all that well. Come to think of it, I remember now that he wasn't her son, just her step son."

Caleb absorbed the new information, adding layers to what they knew and adding questions that needed to be answered.

Chapter 21

The Mastermind was livid. The forger she had hired was dead. That no-good step son of hers had outlived his usefulness. It seemed though that he had tried to throw a monkey wrench into her plans. Look where it landed him! Good riddance! Joshua Logan had been found. It was all falling apart. Her scheme to get rich was in ruins, thanks to that Laycee Bradley. She was ready to kill her, if only she could find her. Where had she run to?

A knock at her business office door startled her. Pulling her face back into the impassive look she always had, she acknowledged her secretary. Behind the woman, Caleb and Ben loomed. A flicker of anger flashed through her eyes and was gone.

Caleb entered, followed by Ben. He said nothing, just stared at her. She stared back, not giving anything away.

"Why, Joy? Why did you do it? Was it the money? Was it the thrill of fooling people?" Caleb's voice had unleashed anger.

She was suddenly afraid. "I don't know what you're talking about. And close the door on your way out. I have a teleconference in 10 minutes."

"No, you don't. You have a conference with us, at the police station. Stand up."

She sat there staring at him. "What?"

"You heard me. Stand up. You're under arrest. Cuff her, Ben." Caleb turned as a heavy glass paperweight hit the door frame. "Add assaulting a police officer to the charge," he told Ben, hearing him read her her rights.

Caleb sighed. They knew why and how Joy had been swindling the elderly and others who weren't so alert. She had made millions in a phony investment scam. That was now in the hands of seasoned investigators and financial people, who were hopeful to return much of the money she had scammed.

Joshua was safe. Now he had to find Laycee

****

Laycee stirred, feeling the warmth of the sun on her face. She felt wood underneath her. It wasn't the same feeling she had had for days. At least she thought it was days. She opened her eyes and closed them just as quickly. The sun was bright. She gradually opened them and just laid there, relishing the warmth after the coldness she had felt. She glanced around. She was free. There were no walls. No windows. No doors.

She sat up and looked around again. She was back to where it had almost started days ago. She was on the dock at the cabin. Her phone was lying beside her.

She picked up the phone and looked at it. It was charged. Very strange.

Hand shaking, she flipped through her contacts and found Liam. She punching in his number hoping he answered and it didn't go to voice mail.

"Hi, you've reached Liam. Leave your name and number."

Laycee sobbed, wanting to speak with him. She tried Leith and got his voice mail too.

She looked up and then once again down at her phone. Trembling she searched and found the number she was looking for.

"Hello?" She heard the warm tenor voice answer.

"Joshua?"

She heard the pause, then "Laycee? Is that you? Where are you? I'm coming."

"Joshua, I'm at the cabin. Come get me. I can't reach Liam or Leith."

"Honey, I'm on my way!" Joshua almost sang the words. He clicked off and then dialed Liam's.

As Liam answered, Joshua was yelling, "She's safe, Liam. She's at the cottage. I'm on my way."

Joshua heard a Praise the Lord and then silence. He knew Liam would be calling Leith.

He dialed Caleb. "Caleb, Laycee called. She's at the cabin. I'm on my way there."

Caleb was yelling at him not to go. With no response from Joshua, he ran from the station, Ben on his heels, barking orders for patrol officers, investigators and paramedics to get there.

The paramedics surrounded Laycee, much to the consternation of her brothers. Joshua paced off to the side. Caleb stood and watched as the investigators probed the area and bagged what might be evidence. The senior paramedic stood and beckoned Caleb over.

Caleb stood at the side of the stretcher, his hand on Laycee's arm. She opened her eyes, and then drifted off. He nodded for them to leave, knowing that the three men who waited would be right behind them. He would get her story later. He looked up, gave a prayer of thanks, and pulled out his phone to call his wife with the good news.

Chapter 22

Laycee looked around her living room. It seemed to be filled with people, all thankful she was safe.

Caleb sat down beside her. "Okay, Laycee, give. What happened?"

"I really don't know. I came out of the police station that day and that's the last I really remember until today. I vaguely remember someone speaking to me and that's it."

"What we figure happened is that Joy Smith had you grabbed. She was behind it all. She had set up phony investments and she thought you had found out about it from one of the seniors. We found the man who was forging documents for her. She removed him once she had no need for him. The two men who ransacked your house—no word on them but I hope they are still alive somewhere and are a lot smarter than they were. The forger had stayed at the Applewood Farm, which is the note you found directing him to go there."

"I guess I'll never really know, will I?"

Ben, who had been on his phone, spoke up. "We do. Joy's estranged step son had found out what she was up to. He knew the violence his mother was capable of and didn't want to see you hurt."

Laycee's eyes studied Ben. "I don't remember her having a step-son."

Ben shook his head. "Peter Adams." Laycee's eyes brightened as she recalled Peter now. "He's been away from here for many years. He had taken to forging documents and from what I am hearing had done a very good job, almost undetectable from the original.

"Joy Smith had set up a scam involving the seniors at the home you volunteered at. She somehow thought you had found out and were gathering documentation to prove it. She had your house ransacked. Peter had stayed at Applewood Farm and had wandered over to your cabin to put in time. He was pretty good at picking locks. Somehow he placed that envelop in that book and moved the books around. That's what you found."

Laycee shook her head. "All this for something I had no idea about? People are strange." Laycee stopped. "Where's my backpack? That brown envelop. I found in it Ella Lang's room one day. She didn't want it, said it wasn't hers. I took it and never looked at it. I actually forgot about sticking it up under the truck seat.

Caleb reached for it and opened it, spending out the documents. They all crowded around him and looked. It was the evidence they needed to seal Joy Smith's doom. There were original documents of Ella's as well as papers showing the attempt to forge her signature. There was also instructions from Joy to Peter on how he was to proceed and what Joy needed in order to set up her scam and gain control of Ella's finances. They had found much more incriminating evidence with the search of Joy's home and office and her financial accounts.

"How did you get these?" Liam asked.

Laycee stared at the papers. "Ella told me to take them. The cleaners found them on the floor in her room. She was adamant they weren't hers. I took a peek and had planned to turn them in. I stuck them under my truck seat and then forgot about them until the accident."

"Why the cryptogram?" Joshua asked.

Ben spoke up. "It really wasn't meant to be one but when Peter lost that envelop that Laycee found in Ella's room, Joy decided that everything thing should be coded. Because she's an accountant, numbers came naturally to her."

"Why was Joshua taken?" Leith wondered.

"No particular reason, other than he was always with Laycee over those days, and they couldn't be sure what he knew. They also couldn't get to Laycee if he was around. They had apparently hired two men to track her and get the documents. We have one of them in jail on unrelated drinking charges and he talked before he was totally sober. His brother has left town."

Laycee sat back down and cuddled Terror in her arms. She sighed, "All this because of money. All this because someone got greedy." She stopped. "But who set me free? Who took me from Joy's house where she had me locked up in a bedroom to the dock at the cabin?"

The men stopped and looked at each other and then at her. That was a good question

"I promise we'll find out," Joshua said, eyes focused on the woman he loved. "The main thing is that God spared you and sent someone."

Ben spoke up. "I did find out. Joy's housekeeper was terrified of Joy, but when she locked Laycee up in the bedroom, she had to do something. She knew Joy's step-son was on to Joy and wanted to help Laycee. She had her husband help Peter move Laycee to the cabin, figuring we would find her, when Joy was arrested."

Liam and Leith shared a glance, then Liam spoke. "You know what Mom and Dad would have said? God is in control. We may never know the full extent of what you went through or were spared, but God values you more than a sparrow."

"What happens with the therapy group now?" Leith asked.

Caleb responded, "The board will be meeting and setting up new officers and new protocols. It will continue."

Laycee nodded, then spoke, "Okay everyone out. I want some me time with Defiant and Terror. Party next week."

"Can't you name that cat anything but Terror?" Leith complained. "She certainly isn't a terror." He ducked the cushion flying at his head as the room emptied to laughter.

Joshua took a look at her, dropped a kiss on her head and left, promising to come back the next day.

Laycee stretched out on the couch, Defiant curled up behind her knees, and Terror perched on top of her. She was home and safe.

<hr>

Epilogue

Two months later, it seemed a dream what she had gone through. Laycee wandered through her house and then stepped out the back door to stand on her deck. The breeze was still warm, for November.

Defiant curled up on her feet, his tri-coloured coat glistening in the sun. Terror perched on her shoulder. She heard the door close behind her and strong arms came around her. She leaned back against Joshua. He had become an almost daily visitor, one she depended on.

Terror decided that Joshua's shoulder made a better perch, higher up, and climbed up on him. She gave his ear a thorough washing and then sat looking around her domain.

"Your cat just washed my ear, you know."

Laycee grinned and nodded.

"Your cat is now talking to me."

Laycee snickered, knowing what was coming.

"Your cat is singing. Singing, do you hear?" Joshua's voice was incredulous. He had never heard a cat sing. Laughter erupted and shook his body.

Terror shot off his shoulder, claws digging in, with a loud meow. The sparrows in the yard scattered. Defiant took off after them, barking, Blues on his heels, with Terror speeding along in a black and white flash.

"Your dog is herding the birds."

Laycee started to laugh, finding it difficult to stop. "He's a Sheltie, a herding dog. Herding dogs herd. He's only doing what comes naturally."

Joshua joined in her laughter. Then, as the evening light dimmed, he sobered.

"Laycee, I am so glad you are safe. You have come to mean the world to me."

She turned to look up at him. "Okay, let's go steady."

He laughed and looked down at her, hugging her close. "You've got it. Going steady, I like that. We'll see where it goes. With you, I know it will be an adventure."

She hugged him. "With you, I know it will be too. With God on our side, we'll make it through."

They stood there for a few minutes, then Laycee spoke. "Ok, we've gone steady. Let's get engaged."

Joshua's laugh echoed through the yard. The two dogs and the cat came back and sat looking up at them. They were certain their humans had just lost it.

Joshua looked down at Laycee, met her eyes, and kissed the woman he had come to love dearly. "I can see it will be a life-long adventure. Can we keep our secret for a while?"

Her brown eyes sparkled as she gazed up at him and hugged him. "Sure, for a day or two." She stood in silence, then said, "God really does care, doesn't He? I look at a sparrow now and remember that He loves and cares for me so much more than one of them. We are His. He has had to teach me that over and over, but during this time especially, it really did make sense."

"That we are, my love. That He does."

Dear Readers:

Thank you for taking the time to read my very first, debut novel. This novel has been bouncing around in my head for years. The first few paragraphs of Chapter 1, where Laycee is pursued and then crashes her truck, are literally taken step by step from a dream. My dreams are suspense novels and I have often woken up scared, but wondering how the story turns out, and sometimes with a scream in my throat. I am an avid reader. The love of books was instilled in me as a child by my Mother, who loved to read, and always gifted books at Christmas, birthdays, and sometimes just because. As an adult, we would race to be the first to read a novel by a favourite author, but ended up taking turns. On the day she graduated to heaven, she literally had a book in her hands just minutes before she was called Home.

I live in a house with three Shetland Sheepdogs, a sable girl named Emma, a tricoloured boy named Liam, and a tricoloured girl named Natalie. They are my world. They add so much enrichment and enjoyment to my life. Of course, a Sheltie had to make his way into the book. Defiant is loosely based on my Liam. Liam really does herd the birds, including the seagulls that fly in from Lake Erie. Added to the mix are two rescue cats. Ceilidh (pronounced Kaylee) is a gray tabby the dogs' breeder found on a highway and saved. I fell in love with this little kitty, who loves to curl up and cuddle. Ciara (pronounced Keera) is a little tuxedo rescue. Terror in the book is based on her. She really does chirp and sing and romp her way through the days,

---

often sleeping on top of me at night. Of course, these two cats are convinced they are Shelties. A man's house is said to be his castle; mine is more a circus at times, but it is my home and sanctuary.

I would like to thank a couple of friends who have taken the time to read through the drafts. Jean West, author in her own right, has read and critiqued my novel and offered valuable support and advice. Thank you, Jean. I enjoy the entertainment that your three Shelties bring to your life. And another dear friend and sister in Christ, Faye Silvestro Kubassek. Thank you, Faye, for being a friend and support over the years and believing in my dream and taking the time to read through the manuscript as well. You are a treasure in my life.

My Mother challenged me one day when I shared about two years before she left us in 2010 that I wanted to write a novel. Her response was "Why don't you". Mom, here's the novel. I just wish you were here today so I could put the very first copy of my very first book in your hands. My Father was quiet but we knew he supported us in our endeavors. I can hear his "You did a wonderful job" in my ear as I write. They were the prayer warriors of our family. That is missed. Cherish the time with your parents and family. It is too short.

We sometimes look at the big picture of life and end up overwhelmed. That is not how God expects us to think. Take a look at the lowly sparrow, despised by many, living through all kinds of conditions. God cares for these sparrows. Yet in His word, it is very clearly stated that we are so much more to Him. Trust Him in your daily walk. You're never alone.

———

123

Once again, thank you. Enjoy the adventures of Laycee and Joshua. I used to snicker when authors would comment on how the plot changed and characters would enter a book and take over. Not any more. That is exactly what happened. The plot of the book is not what I started out with. Caleb was to be a minor character but law enforcement ended up needing a strong person. Characters changed from villain to friend. The constant was God's caring.

As I end, I can hear Liam and Leith clamouring in the background, demanding that their stories be told, and so, the adventure will continue with the Bradley siblings.

www.ingramcontent.com/pod-product-compliance
Lightning Source LLC
Chambersburg PA
CBHW070515200726
48293CB00007B/2544